DEAD WEIGHT: The Tombs

A Tale of the Faerie War

Kat
Can you
out run
fate?

By:
M Todd Gallowglas

M Todd

9 8 7 6 5 4 3 2 1 0

For Alice LaPlante

Without you Dead Weight *would have remained a simple action-adventure novelette lost within itself. Thank you for guiding me to the rich and terrible world surrounding this story.*

DEAD WEIGHT: The Tombs

Acknowledgements

First and foremost, I have to thank my wife, Robin, for her patience and understanding with the collective story of *Dead Weight*. She was the first person to read the original novelette in September of 2007. She's seen it through all its rough edges, and believe me, it's had quite a few. Even at times when I felt this story was too big for my meager talent, she kept at me, asking, "When are you going to finish *Dead Weight?*" Thanks, as always, for believing.

Second, I have to thank my editor, whose patience comes in only slightly behind Robin's. I'm keeping my editor on the edge with this one, not just in scope, but we're both out of our comfort zones. Thanks, as always for taking these jumbles of words I spew onto the page into a story.

Mathew Clark Davidson. We didn't see eye to eye on a lot of things when I was taking classes from him. This installment would not exist if he hadn't given a writing prompt with, "The character has to solve the problem with fire." He was also the one who gave me the first glimpse of how massive the world of Dead Weight is.

I'd be remiss if I didn't mention my cohort in crime, and the true foundation of the Genre Underground, Christopher Kellen, for the cover and helping to keep me relatively sane while I raced to the finish line on this one.

Thanks to John McDonnell for translating the Irish. You'll have your work cut out for you in future installments.

Joe, Hoover, Victor, and all the awesome guys out at the Vacaville Airsoft field for being my weekend brothers in arms. Being able to head out to the field and face simulated death on a regular basis has really stepped up my game in writing fight scenes.

Brian and Cody (and sometimes Jenni) for putting up with me during Wednesday night writing night.

You should all bow before the folks at my two local Starbucks for keeping me well-caffeinated, as they have with so many books.

And a final thank you in two parts. First to Tim O'Brien for writing "The Things they Carried," and second, to Paul Bailiff for assigning that story in Fundamentals of Creative Reading. These were the butterfly's wings that instigated the storm that is *Dead Weight*.

Forward
By Damon Stone

This is an amazing time to be a fan. At no other point in history has there been such a popular acceptance of geek and nerd culture coupled with the ability for independent artists to get their work out in front of the public. To me, being a geek is about loving what you love regardless of how others view you and being nerd is about immersing yourself in whatever it is you are passionate about. Musicians, illustrators, actors, game designers, and writers have been able to use technology to stand the producer/consumer paradigm on its head. That you hold this creation is proof of that. Without having to rely on corporate giants to decide what is worth presenting to the consumer, each artist, in this case M Todd Gallowglas, can present their material directly to the consumer. That gives **us** the power. We don't have to read, play, watch, or listen to things created for the lowest common denominator or an overly broad and unfocused demographic, we can find exactly what we want, and give our money directly to the artist. I love this symbiotic relationship. If you want to immerse yourself in a story of a junkie bard veteran from a war where San Francisco was the front lines in an Unseelie incursion, you can. And believe me, I do.

Dead Weight is a fantastic world, literally. As the story unfolds, you start to feel that weight settle upon you, a hidden world reveals implacable foes and a war, somehow fought against all odds to a standstill. The history of this alternate universe slowly reveals itself and draws you further in, each step wrapping you more firmly in its grip. The war, its aftermath, and the prospect of an uneasy peace, could have been ripped from our own headlines – it invites us to both lose ourselves in the fantasy and to examine an uncomfortable reality. The best of fantasy and science fiction is not about escapism, but challenges us to look at ourselves, our society, and reexamine our beliefs. This world and this author do just that, not heavy-handedly, but with elegance – it creeps up on you. I like that.

Damon Stone

Game Designer, Fantasy Flight Games

DEAD WEIGHT:
The Tombs

...while I discovered that my own exploration of Faerieland had only just begun. In the countryside, the old stories seemed to come alive around me; the faeries were a tangible aspect of the landscape, pulses of spirit, emotion, and light. They "insisted" on taking form under my pencil, emerging on the page before me cloaked in archetypal shapes drawn from nature and myth. I'd attracted their attention, you see, and they hadn't finished with me yet.

— Brian Froud

Now begin in the middle, and later learn the beginning; the end will take care of itself.

— " 'Repent Harlequin!' Said the Ticktockman" Harlan Ellison

DEAD WEIGHT: The Tombs

EPILOGUE, THE FIRST

If my doctor told me I had only six minutes to live, I wouldn't
brood.
I'd type a little faster.
– Isaac Asimov

Be grateful for whoever comes,
because each has been sent as a guide from beyond.
— Rumi

Max blinked down at the metal blade sticking out of his chest just to the left of his sternum. He couldn't tell if it was a sword or spear or…well…did it really matter at this point?

Ha! He thought. *Point! Good one.*

He might have laughed if he hadn't been coughing up blood all over his chin at that moment. Or, maybe that *is* laughing when you have something metal sticking through your chest.

That shouldn't have been possible. Not with his gray T-shirt on. Max closed his eyes, hoping things would be different when he o-pened them again. A futile effort, yeah. Dying men will grasp for anything they can to suck wind just a little while longer. Max o-pened his eyes. The bloody mess of the blood-covered point still stuck out of his chest. Odd though…it didn't hurt even close to how much he would have expected.

Blood dripped from the tip – Max tried to ignore the fact that it was his blood – onto the newspapers, parchments, and books that covered the table. It was a few drops at first, and then the flood-gates opened. He remembered a time back in the war, marching a-long with a platoon of Marines, when he saw a waterfall that same color spilling down a cliffside at sunset.

Glancing over his shoulder, Max saw a petite figure in a deep gray long coat, complete with a hood. Shadows hid most of the face inside that hood, but he saw a narrow chin and thin lips painted in gray lipstick matching the coat. Like pillars, two platinum-blond braids fell out of the hood and framed that chin.

"I know you," Max said.

The girl nodded. Or was she a woman? Max couldn't remember.

It might be the blood loss, but Max couldn't remember how long it had been since he thought of himself as "Max." Years, maybe, perhaps a decade or more. Then again, it might have been only a few weeks. The room spun around him as his head grew dizzy with blood loss. He remembered one of the foundations of the Old Knowledge he hadn't considered in a long, long while: *Time becomes fluid and mutable at the slightest touch of Faerie.*

"Is that all?" Max asked.

"That should do it," she replied with a whisper, and backed away.

As she retreated, blending into the shadows, the blade slid out of his chest. *Holy fucking Christ Buddha badger fuck*, Max screamed in his mind. That hurt more than he had words to describe, and he owned a lot of words and had used those words to describe a lot of things.

A moment later, the girl was gone.

Max waited for his life to flash before his eyes.

Unfortunately, human lives have too much extraneous crap filling up the meaningless moments for a whole life to flash before a dying person's eyes. Rather, people must see what is most important to them. Max had spent the better part of his life twisting and manipulating names and words, so that's what came to him, names, words, and titles: Max, Lies, Boy Scout, Champion, Friend, Hero, Traitor, Father, Son, Writer, Journalist, and the one he hated most of all, Bard.

Bard...Bard...Bard...a blessing and curse to all who held that title.

Eyelids half-closed, the waterfall slowing to a trickle, Max saw one piece of paper untouched by his blood on the far corner of the table. Somehow, not a single drop touched that piece of paper. He loved the sight of an unblemished page, full of infinite possibilities of what a writer or artist might create. If only he had time to fill that page, but alas, it was too late. Then, an odd quote came to mind, a quote by Lao Tzu: *Time is a created thing.* Paring that with the Old Knowledge, *Time becomes fluid and mutable at the slightest touch of Faerie,*

Max understood he had one chance to save his life. It was a desperate move, but moments like these are the perfect time for desperate moves. And perhaps because it was such a desperate move, he also thought it might give him the chance to set things right.

Max dabbed his right index finger into the wound on his chest.

Funny, he thought, *I thought that would hurt more.*

He slumped forward, placed his bloodied finger on the paper, and wrote four letters.

S-T-O-P.

Everything did, including the blood flowing out of his chest.

A scrap of paper poked out from under the sheet containing those bloody letters. Max took the scrap and read the words written on it in a curving, sweeping hand, in Irish, no less...

Tá sé in am scéal Tommy a chríochnú.
Translation:
Time to finish Tommy's story.

Since he had nothing but time, Max took out his pen and the beat-up journal where he'd started Tommy's story and started writing.

THE TOUR:
A Prologue of Sorts

...but nothing is ever lost nor can be lost.
The body sluggish, aged, cold, the ember left from earlier fires shall duly flame
again.
– Walt Whitman

How should we be able to forget those ancient myths that are at the beginning of
all peoples, the myths about dragons that at the last moment turn into
princesses; perhaps all the dragons of our lives are princesses who are only
waiting to see us once beautiful and brave. Perhaps everything terrible is in its
deepest being something helpless that wants help from us.

So you must not be frightened if a sadness rises up before you larger than any
you have ever seen; if a restiveness, like light and cloudshadows, passes over your
hands and over all you do. You must think that something is happening with
you, that life has not forgotten you, that it holds you in its hand; it will not let
you fall. Why do you want to shut out of your life any uneasiness, any miseries,
or any depressions? For after all, you do not know what work these conditions
are doing inside you.
— Letters to a Young Poet, Rainer Maria Rilke

Military historians argue the reasons the enemy devastated the United States so much in the early years of the Faerie War. In hindsight it really shouldn't be that big a mystery; the United States simply forgot too much of the Old Knowledge. If they hadn't, they would have been much better prepared.

From the moment the white man displaced the first Native American tribe, the United States sowed the seeds of its later inability to deal with the aggression from Faerie in the middle of the Twenty-First Century. Only the artists and those who lived on the fringes of society seemed to remember, and we know how the U.S. felt about *those people*. Thus, America lacked the resources to stem the early onslaught. Perhaps that is why the Unseelie chose to make the United States the focal point of its reentry into the human world.

15

As it is in the wake of all great conflicts of the modern era, now that the Faerie War is over, people yearn and strive to recapture the cultural mythology of all our forefathers and to make sense of a war with an enemy that we are unlikely to ever make sense of.

Some people study, spending time on the internet, in libraries, and delving into dark corners of occult and arcane bookstores, searching for the minutest details of faerie lore and legend to better deal with the world as it is after the war. Others, those who are not so academically minded, take tours.

Every day, thousands of people take pictures of the blackened crater in Washington, D.C. where the original Capitol used to stand. The crater still smokes today. They visit the fortress that sprang up in Central Park that took the military over three years of constant siege to capture. Just recently, the air space above and inside the Grand Canyon has become safe enough for people to fly through to see the last strongholds of the fey in our world.

However, unlike many previous wars, the most popular tours aren't of battle sites. This was a war unlike any remembered, save in myths and legends. The most important conflicts weren't fought by soldiers. To truly understand the Faerie War, people flock to see those places where visionaries created works of art striving to repel the invasion before it began.

One of the most popular tours is in the San Francisco Bay Area. This tour, thanks to magic left over from the Faerie War, teleports people from site to site to see the artwork of a girl, a girl who saw through the cracks in reality before any other person in the world. She was the first to fight with her spray paint cans and paint brushes and pastels. Her best efforts came to nothing, because of the best of intentions of a boy who only wanted to help make his community a nicer place.

The tour begins in the girl's childhood bedroom. When people pay their twenty dollars in the foyer of the house she grew up in, the underpaid state park employee hands them a set of headphones. Each of these devices narrates the tour, beginning from the moment one reaches the top of the stairs and turns left into the bedroom. The voice is a pleasant male voice, containing a slight tremor.

"Let us begin with the south wall. It contains pictures that the artist..." – nowhere in the tour or any literature is the girl named; names have power, even after so much time, to affect things in the world that are better left alone; so, as it is with every such tour, she is referred to always as *the artist* – "…colored and painted in pre-school and kindergarten." These contain images, different colors blending together, and of stick-figure people fighting stick-figure monsters.

"You may notice that, even in their simplicity, something about them draws you. Occasionally when the light hits a picture just right, or if perhaps, you look at a picture from just the right angle, those simple pictures might seem to move a little bit. If you do manage to notice this effect, keep it to yourself. Any time someone tries to call this to the attention of someone else, the effect stops, and the magic of that moment is lost.

"Let us turn to the west wall. These are works the artist created in elementary school. You will notice the increasing complexity and that she painted creatures that we take for granted now – in all their alien wonder. Some of the pictures are of familiar forms: dragons, unicorns, elves, pixies, sprites, and ogres. Others are bizarre creatures with a single leg, or three arms, or eyes all around their heads. The impressive thing isn't that she painted these things, even though she painted them even before the war; it's that her artwork, even at the young age that she created it, fills viewers with such wonder that they feel like a child hearing their first fairy tales again. Don't you agree?

"Allow me to draw your attention to a specific picture: two rows in from the left and five down. The one displaying a scene with a faerie lady standing over a knight on one knee."

The work is done in watercolor paint with alternating long and short strokes. The background is blended shades of green, brown, and yellow. The lady is dressed in red and silver, and the knight's armor is gray and black. The lady holds a sword with a blue blade, and she's touching the knight's shoulder with it.

"Some people claim that while looking at the lady for more than a few moments that they can feel a warm breeze in their hair and the sword's leather hilt pressing into their hands. Others will tell you that if you look at the knight long enough that you'll feel the cold edge of a blade caressing the side of your neck. Do you? Don't answer yet if you are skeptical of such things. Look for a moment without thinking too much about it, and you may feel what the artist intended you to feel.

"By now, you have no doubt noticed the centerpiece of this wall has several ribbons next to it. These are the only official prizes her work has ever received."

This picture of a dragon was colored with crayons on lined binder paper. The thirty-four vertical blue lines and the one horizontal red line are this picture's only background. The face of a dragon fills three-quarters of the paper. The scales begin with light green, shaded with gray on the outside of the beast's snout and darkening to almost black in the center. Its eyes are gold with flecks of red. Its lips curve upward at the very edges, as if this creature understands more about the viewer than the viewer does.

"Can you feel the warmth of the creature's breath on your face? Do you hear a subtle chuckling in the back of your mind? If not, don't feel bad. Not everyone does."

On the north wall the work gets more elaborate. These are the paintings – real paintings rendered on canvas – that she did in her high school years.

"Notice how these paintings show noble faerie lords and ladies hunting in woods of weeping willows with watery tears where the leaves should be and also shows epic battles between the two ruling courts of Arcadia: the Seelie and Unseelie. See how the artist chose to represent the Seelie court with bright colors and depicts them as knights in radiant armor, while she portrays the Unseelie court as grim and dark, with the relatively human-looking of them possessing demonic features. At this point, we all know these are not accurate portrayals of these creatures. The fey do not conform to humans ideals of good and evil, light and dark. They are alien creatures whose morality is something far removed from human ethics. Many people have wondered why the artist chose to portray the courts in such a way, but without being able to speak directly to her, the mystery will remain."

The centerpiece of this wall is an oil painting that the girl cre0-ated during a special summer school for the arts. It's four feet by three feet and depicts a scene where two faerie armies clash around two mortal champions. Seelie knights ride unicorns and griffins into the battle, while the Unseelie ride giant buzzards and dragons. The infantries of both sides clash with sword and spear and claw and fang. The air throughout the battle is charged with magical energy. Even with all this chaos, there remains a wide circle around the two mortals who are playing a game of chess, seemingly undistracted by the conflict that rages around them. While standing near this wall, tourists can almost hear the trees crying, the tromp of unicorn, and the faint screams of the wounded on the battlefield amidst the clash of steel on steel. They smell of blood and fresh loam, and the chill wind of forests older than anything we know on earth tickles the hair of the arm. And underneath all that, they hear the tick, tick, tick, of the chess clock and one of the players sigh in displeasure at his opponent's previous move.

"This painting has drawn people to ask many questions: Why are these two people playing a game in the middle of this fighting? Do they even know the battle is there? Which of these two scenes is real? Are they even in the same place? Why do the fey leave them alone to play their game?"

At this point, the tour jumps to other locations. After the girl left high school, she became a graffiti artist. Her work appears in many secret and out-of-the-way places throughout the San Francisco Bay Area. Her paintings appear in tunnels, under overpasses, on walls of alleyways. These works generally take up the entirety of whatever surface she used for a canvas. People are ushered through the locations quickly, because the physical sensations felt in the presence of the works can become addicting. One painting in an alley in downtown San Francisco depicts a riverbed where a group of nyads (a type of water fey) and dryads (fey spirits bound into trees) are singing and playing harps, lutes, and pan pipes. This alley is always seventy-three degrees Fahrenheit, no matter the time of day or the weather, and the faint whisper of a song can be heard as if a radio is playing at low volume just around the corner. The side effects of this painting have required round-the-clock security to turn away any of the homeless who try to squat here.

The voice in the headphones accompanies the tourists to each location on the tour as both moderator and one-sided conversationalist.

Eventually the tour returns to the girl's house, and the visitors can look behind the curtain of the final wall, the east wall, which is dominated by a single piece. This is a painting of a door with a single, old-fashioned keyhole.

"This concludes our regular tour. For the expanded tour, which allows you to look through the keyhole, please see information desk for the release form and appropriate donation rates. Thank you. Have a great day, and we hope to see you again."

That is where the recorded voice stops.

Not everyone has the courage or the curiosity to sign the release and look through the keyhole. These days, most people understand that exposing themselves to anything having to do with faerie magic is a gamble and that the odds are not in their favor.

For those who do sign the waver and look through the keyhole, most will only see a beautiful, though very small, picture of the girl's parents' bedroom. It also shows her parents, dead always in the way the viewer fears most to die: hanging, burning, murder, sickness – it doesn't matter what the fear, the magic of this tiny painting always knows. However, a few very rare and unique individuals see what the girl saw. That's why this tour and others like it remain open, and will remain open so long as the government stands. Tours like these are the surest way to find artists who can take up where the girl left off.

This bears some explanation.

The barrier between realities is not equal in all places. Sometimes cracks form between one world and another. These cracks usually happen in out-of-the-way or secret, hidden places: under beds, behind furniture, in backyards hidden behind that tangle of bushes and shrubs that never seems to get pruned; and in places where children and artists gather: galleries, playgrounds, jungle gyms, avant-garde coffee houses; or where the human mind slips from the realm of normal perceptions: mental wards, crack houses, Burning Man. These cracks and holes are usually too small to see, mostly because the average human is too busy with the minutia of their banal life to notice anything of true wonder. But then, they are not the gifted ones; they are not the artists, the madmen, that the rest of humanity looks at whom they shake their heads with pity. "Normal" people don't understand these people or the pity they feel for them. They cannot comprehend that by seeing through the cracks in the world these gifted and mad artists destined for lives of hardship, unhappiness, and alienation.

In the moment just before most "normal" people looking through the keyhole would grasp what is it to live with the gift and curse these artists possess, they look away – and most of them forget.

Most.

Those few who do not look away soon find themselves creating their own works of art, whether painting, music, poetry, sculpting, etc. They see the cracks between the worlds. They see into Faerie and all its breathtaking wonder, madness, and horror. It is a timeless land that knows nothing of death. It is a realm of gnarled gardens, mountains of half-gnawed bones, and of primeval forests, lush and dark in both beauty and savagery. These forests writhe alongside concrete jungles, thick with artfully bent metal and snowflakes of broken glass. Almost-Victorian estates rest upon shorelines scattered with carcasses of sailing vessels, thousands of ships carved from the fossilized remains of giant beasts that dwarf the greatest of dinosaurs. Satyrs and centaurs frolic in meadows of red grass where the heads of human babies grow in place of dandelions. Those who have the talent to see beyond static reality take up their art as champions against the fey who still seek to threaten this world. The war may be over, but as it has for millennia, the threat of Faerie remains. Only this time, several gates between Earth and Faerie remain open. Because of that, this tour, with a tiny picture inside that keyhole, remains open in the hope that enough mad and brilliant artists will awaken to fight and hold the Unseelie at bay.

UNINVITED GUESTS

Oh, for a muse of fire that would ascend the brightest heaven of invention...
— <u>Henry V</u>, William Shakespeare

A very little key will open a very heavy door.
— <u>Hunted Down</u>, Charles Dickens

One of the stops on the girl's tour is in the Tombs. Before the Faerie War, the Tombs used to be the Mission District and Potrero Hill. Now, it's a no-man's-land surrounding the largest portal to Faerie in the whole world. Because of the dangers lurking throughout the Tombs and its proximity to the gate, this spray-painted mural of a fiery redheaded girl wearing a coat of peacock feathers greeting a man in golden armor as he steps out of a nimbus of light is the tour's only stop in this neighborhood. The government doesn't want to pay for the security required to keep the other three known locations of the girl's art safe.

The dingy and run-down buildings get only intermittent power at best, adding another challenge to security. The human squatters and transients who live in the Tombs use battery powered lanterns, when they can get batteries. When they can't, they go without. Most consider the risk of fire too great. However, candlelight does flicker without fail in one window, no matter the time, day or night. Even with the risk of fire, none of the residents do anything about it. They've learned that the man who lives in that particular apartment will not allow anything to happen to that continuous flame. That candle belongs to a man who met the artist girl once when they both were very young and both had the best of intentions.

The man woke and rubbed the grime from his eyes, feeling much older than his twenty-eight years. He heaved a breath that was somewhere between a sigh and a growl. His high had faded too soon, but then, it was always too soon. He had a name, had had many names, but he only used one name now. Those few times he spoke to other people, he told them to call him Boy Scout. He'd earned the name in what felt like a lifetime ago. Hell, he'd even deserved it back then. Now, he kept the name for irony's sake, and as another way to punish himself.

Boy Scout took his hands away from his eyes. A flame danced on top of a candle set on the crate in the center of the room. That flame was his security. When Boy Scout had to wander from home, he always had a Zippo in hand – not just with him, but in his hand. He'd stroke its smooth surface with his right thumb, the one with the tattoo for the Chinese character for south.

He flung his blanket aside. The chill of the night air hit his naked skin, but he didn't care. Well, he did care. San Francisco air in the late fall was chilly as the best of times. He just knew he wouldn't care in about a minute. Once a fresh shot of heroin worked its way through his system, he wouldn't care about anything...again.

Crawling out of the lumpy futon, Boy Scout's hand came down on a patch of mold. His stomach churned and his throat choked off some rising bile. He wiped his hand on the blanket. His pants lay on the floor next to the futon. He contemplated pulling them on for a-bout a second. They served no purpose in getting high, so he crawled past them on the way to the crate.

He picked up the candle, gently as he could, to set it on the floor. Just as he had it in his hand and away from the stable surface, a siren wailed from outside – a rare sound in the Tombs. He jumped and dropped the candle. The room darkened. Boy Scout felt as if plunged into a tub of ice water. He scrambled back to his pants and fished the Zippo out of the front right pocket. A few frantic heartbeats later, he was back at the candle. He picked it up with his left hand and almost chewed through his upper lip as he relit it. When the flame returned light to the apartment, Boy Scout breathed easily again. He set the candle on the floor, very carefully this time, titled the crate, and pulled a leather toiletry kit out from underneath it.

Moments later, he had one end of a black leather belt wrapped around his left arm. His teeth clamped down on the other end. The syringe in his right hand waited for the bulging vein. After that he'd go into that place where he didn't care what he remembered.

"Hey, baby," a voice called from the far corner. "You going to share some of that, right?"

A girl sat on the futon, the blanket wrapped around her under-neath the arms, exposing bare shoulders. Boy Scout wondered if he ever knew her name. She might have been as young as thirteen, maybe even twelve – life in the Tombs had a tendency to age people fast. Despite that, her skin was pale and clean, and even though her blond hair clung to her face and stuck out at odd angles on top and behind her ears, it wasn't from lack of cleanliness. She looked and glowed of sex. Still, even though she smelled cleaner than anyone Boy Scout had spoken to in years – he remembered that much about her from the last few hours – she had the hollow, sunken eyes and tight cheek bones of a professional junkie. Last time Boy Scout looked in a mirror, he saw a face like that looking back.

"Fuck off," Boy Scout snarled without removing the belt from between his teeth.

Three sharp knocks echoed on the door as he was about to slide the needle into his arm.

"I'll get it," the girl said.

"No!"

She ignored him, getting up from the moldy mattress and crossing to the door.

"I said…" Boy Scout's voice trailed off when he noticed all thirteen locks were open. His mouth hung open for a moment, releasing the belt, before he added, "Shit."

This was bad. Beyond bad. Like don't-cross-the-fucking-streams level of disastrous.

Boy Scout tried to stop her. He tried to stand and turn around at the same time. Funny thing with being on the tail end of a good night doped out of his mind, his body couldn't keep up with his intentions. He dropped the syringe as the floor rose up to meet him. The syringe hit the floor and shattered as he wound up face down on a section of floor that smelled of piss. The fragmented glass sparkled next to the candle, and Boy Scout lost his focus in the way the candlelight reflected off the tiny shards of broken glass.

The front door creaked open.

Oh, yeah. Cross-the-streams bad.

"Thanks, bitch."

It took Boy Scout a moment to register those words. The accent was a thick, heavy brogue, and the voice grated like steel wool on a chalkboard.

The girl gasped. Something that sounded like cracking knuckles, only louder, echoed in the room. That would be her neck; it wasn't the first time Boy Scout had heard that sound. The image of his best friend's head twisted at an impossible angle formed in his mind. Something heavy hit the floor, probably her body. What had they offered her to open the door? The runes all around both the door and windows made sure any creature of pure faerie blood couldn't come in without help – Boy Scout knew the old rules a-bout those kinds of things, and he played them to his absolute best advantage. Whatever the offer, she must have gotten it, or she'd still be alive. They couldn't kill her without making good on their half of the deal. Another rule.

"Time to kick the habit, Boy Scout," the ear-grating voice said. Again, with the brogue, it took Boy Scout a moment to process the words. "Oberon has a job for you."

A chorus of cruel laughter filled the room. Boy Scout couldn't tell how many, but he figured at least three…maybe more.

"Fuck off."

Yeah, he'd just said the same thing to the girl, but really, do people expect a junkie to have a dazzling array of witty retorts and snappy comebacks?

He picked up the needle from the broken syringe. Stabbing himself through the tattoo on his right index finger, he dove for the candle. His blood snuffed out the flame, completing the ritual. The smoke curling in the air from the wick held its own light, as if the light from the candle flame had transformed into smoke. In truth, it was a touch of Faerie magic bound into the tattoo. Instead of waft-ing toward the ceiling, the smoke floated above the filth-covered floor and wafted toward the closet.

A pair of rough hands lifted Boy Scout to his feet.

The closet door fell off its hinges and hit the floor with a crash. Rather than revealing a closet, the threshold opened onto a meadow of soot and ash surrounded by flaming, evergreen-shaped trees. The smell of smoldering campfires filled the room, and the temperature increased by about ten degrees. Then *she* stepped into view before the fiery scene. Her flaming hair – not red, *flaming* – whipped in the wind that flowed into the room from the world beyond the door. She wore a jacket of peacock feathers; the center of each eye held a tiny, flickering flame. Underneath the jacket, she had an orange T-shirt with the words *Keep calm and grab a lantern* in letters as black as her cargo pants and leather motorcycle boots.

"Gentlemen," Boy Scout said, "meet Cendrine South."

"Good morning," Cendrine said, stepping across the threshold.

The fiery trees and blackened ground faded back into just a closet, but the temperature continued to rise.

"Put him down."

The floor rose up to meet Boy Scout. His breath slammed out of his chest on impact.

Why were people always so literal with things like that?

Boy Scout lay gasping, waiting for it to be over. Something screamed. It wasn't Cendrine. She *didn't* scream. Ever.

"Get up and get in the fight!" Cendrine yelled.

Boy Scout pulled off a small leather pouch from around his neck, yanked the drawstrings open, and dumped the powder into his mouth. The stuff looked like dried and ground cow shit laced with red pop rocks. As soon as it touched his tongue, the powder transformed into a sweet liquid that slid down his throat like warm brandy. When it reached Boy Scout's stomach, the potions purged any lingering drugs from his system.

He crushed garbage and trash as he rolled across the floor. The glass from the shattered syringe cut into his back, and then, rolling onto his front, he pinned one of his testicles between his thigh and the floor. Boy Scout clenched his teeth against the pain. Without the fog of drugs clouding his mind, neurons fired through over-familiar synaptic pathways. That's when Boy Scout realized he was heading for the wrong corner. That particular hidey hole wasn't likely to help against the faerie. Twisting and rolling, he changed directions and scrambled to the southwest corner of the room.

The floorboards behind him vibrated with a heavy impact. As he crawled away, Boy Scout glanced back. One of his would-be captors strained to pry a firefighter's axe out of the floor. Only changing directions had saved him from losing a leg, or worse. Once upon a time, that would have terrified Boy Scout into inaction. Now, his skin tingled as adrenaline pulsed through his body, and the instinct to kill or be killed took hold of his reflexes.

Boy Scout reached the corner, pressed down on the knot in one of the floorboards, and the board popped open. He thrust his hands inside the alcove and grabbed two bags – one was dark brown suede, the other purple velvet – from the top of his small pile of treasures. He flung his arms outward, sending the contents of both pouches, iron shavings and tiny silver crosses, across the room.

The guy with the axe got a face full of the worst of it. He dropped to his knees, clawing and scratching at his face. Boy Scout kicked him in the face. The attacker's head snapped back, sending his hat flying as he pitched backward and sprawled on the floor.

Boy Scout stared at the hat that had flopped down in the middle of his shoddy apartment. Even with what little light filtered in from outside, he knew what the hat was and what it meant. His stomach sank and he swallowed to keep the bile down as he looked up, fearing what he would see.

Cendrine wove her way between the other five invaders. The tallest of them stood no more than four and a half feet high. Each was about half as wide at the shoulders as he was tall. Wiry black hair sprouted from the necks and cuffs of their tattered, three-piece, double-breasted suits. Their iron-shod boots dug gouges in the wooden floor, but some spell or enchantment must be keeping the boots silent. They carried bone cudgels and firefighter's axes. Each one wore a hat just like the one that had caught Boy Scout's attention. Each hat resembled a Scottish Tam O'Shanter, only without the little ball on top, and each cap was deep red and dripping wet.

Powries. Known to popular folklore as Red Caps. Unseelie monsters that reveled in the fear and misery they caused when they used fresh human blood to maintain the color of their hats. Back in the war, U.S. forces had taken to calling them "Samsons." Their power lies in the hat. If the cap dries, the Powrie dies. The wetter the hat, soaked in human blood, the stronger the Powrie. Boy Scout wondered how many of the tenants of this building had died tonight. Powries were one of the most resilient and terrifying of all dark faeries. He'd heard of whole platoons dying, to the man, trying to take down a single Powrie. Now he had six in his apartment. The iron wouldn't do anything against them. At least not with their caps dripping with all that fresh blood. Until such time as that changed religious trappings were their only real defense, but the tiny crosses would only serve as momentary distractions. Yeah, they'd hurt, but Boy Scout only had the one bag, and that was spent. He could think of only one surefire way to incapacitate them long enough for Cendrine to kill them. If Boy Scout remained alive long enough to see it through.

The Powrie that Boy Scout had just kicked rolled over to its hands and knees. It glared up at him and gave him a wide grin.

"I'm going to bleed you through your feet," it said, "soak my hat in your blood over the course of days."

"Thanks, but I'll pass," Boy Scout said, as he backed away from the feral creature.

Boy Scout struggled to remember something that might be enough to keep them down long enough to tell Cendrine how to beat them. A passage came to him from one of his dad's favorite movies.

"The path of the righteous man is beset on all sides by the inequities of the selfish and the tyranny of evil men."

The Powrie facing him laughed, a deep, gravely sound, as it lumbered to its feet. Boy Scout decided he'd be perfectly happy never hearing the sound again.

He kept quoting. *"Blessed is he, who in the name of charity and good-will, shepherds the weak…"*

The Powrie stepped forward, completely the opposite of the expected reaction. Boy Scout quickened his backpedaling and his speaking so his words almost blended together.

"…through the valley of darkness for he is truly his brother's keeper and the finder of lost children."

"Love that movie, too," the Powrie said, stalking toward Boy Scout.

"Ah, shit. That's right."

Boy Scout recalled that particular monologue wasn't an actual quote from Ezekiel 25:17. He also remembered he'd learned that the hard way once before. But by this time, he had something else.

"The Lord is my shepherd. I shall not want. He maketh me to lie down in green pastures."

The Powries screamed. The sound was a mix of a pig being slaughtered and a buzz saw cutting though ice. They dropped their cudgels and axes and pressed their meaty hands to their ears.

"Cendrine," Boy Scout shouted, "dry the caps." Then, continuing his impromptu sermon, he sprinted across the room. *"He leads me beside still waters; He restores my soul. He leads me in paths of righteousness for His name's sake."*

A nimbus of light appeared around Cendrine. The temperature rose steadily. At first it was no worse than a crowded movie theater without any air-conditioning, then a sauna. In a matter of heartbeats it would be hot as a pottery kiln.

Boy Scout dove out of the window and sprawled onto the rusty fire escape. Metal groaned as bolts holding it to the building's outer wall strained under his weight. He realized that he should have tested it a long time ago. He imagined himself laying naked, splattered all over the street below.

He wasn't a man of faith, even though religious trappings, especially from Catholicism, had such a strong effect on the fey, but this didn't keep him from praying, "Please hold, please hold, please hold," as he laced his fingers around the rusted metal and his entire body tensed for the fall. He didn't know what he was actually praying for: to keep from falling or to not be known as the guy who died naked in the street due to a faulty fire escape.

The structure held. Boy Scout's atheism returned.

"More scripture!" Cendrine yelled.

Now that Boy Scout had really gotten going, more passages he'd memorized back in the war rose from the depths of his memory. He lifted his head level with the window's bottom. Heat flowed out of the window like an oven door. "*Even though I walk through the valley of the shadow of death, I fear no evil; for You are with me; Your rod and Your staff, they comfort me.*" The screams lowered, sounding now like the whimpers of newborn puppies.

"*Surely goodness and mercy shall follow me all the days of my life; and I shall dwell in the house of the Lord forever.*"

A few moments later, Boy Scout heard nothing, and the heat coming out of the window subsided.

In the brief moment of quiet, Boy Scout heard faint singing coming from down the street. He only caught a few words before the singer walked too far out of ear shot. What he had heard, "...beggar than a king, and I'll tell you the reason why..." sent a shudder across his whole body.

As soon as he thought the room would be manageable, Boy Scout shook the sound of that song out of his head and crawled back through the window.

Cendrine stood in the center of the room, holding a pair of his jeans and glaring at him. At least her hair had gone back to being hair. It was still deep red, but it wouldn't singe him if he got too close.

Cendrine tossed his jeans at him. "Have some sense of decency."

Boy Scout snatched the pants out of the air. "Wasn't expecting company."

As he pulled his jeans on, Boy Scout took stock of the apartment. It was the first time in a long, long time that he'd done so sober. Did he really live like this?

The Powries lay in awkward, contorted positions. Each hat now looked brittle and dried brown as opposed to dripping and deep blood red. Cendrine searched through their pockets and under their hats.

"Ugh," Boy Scout grunted.

"You have no room to judge anything I do," Cendrine replied, as she lifted another formerly red cap from a dead faerie.

Boy Scout opened his mouth to make some poignant commentary on a lack of knowledge of how sanitary Red Caps were when it came to their hair care practices. They spent centuries, sometimes millennia, soaking their hats in human blood and never cleaning them. Couldn't possibly be healthy.

Cendrine glanced at the shattered syringe, and back at him. She didn't say anything else. She didn't have to. She looked like the parent of a teenager that can't manage to stay out of trouble. The irony was not lost on him.

As Cendrine searched the attackers, Boy Scout went over to his bed, lifted the edge of the mattress, and picked up the iron railroad spike he kept hidden there. It warmed his palm, almost to the point of burning him. He wrapped the spike in a discarded shirt, and crawled a few feet to one of the Powries.

The faerie's breath came in ragged gasps. It looked up at him, then shifted its gaze to the railroad spike...the *iron* railroad spike.

"Hi," Boy Scout said. "Probably been a while since your cap was dry enough that you had to worry about something like this, right?"

"Wait." Its face contorted as it spoke. Good. It deserved some pain before the end. "You're a bard. You can do no harm."

"Sure I can," Boy Scout said. "You broke the Law of Hospitality. I'm just exercising Host Right for your transgressions."

"We are invaders, not your guests," the faerie said. "Kill us and lose your powers."

Boy Scout grabbed the Red Cap by the hair and turned its face toward the door.

"See that?" Boy Scout asked. "It's my door. It's got a threshold. Strangers stay on the far side. Only friends and guests come on this side. If you thought to look, the bottom of the door has a tiny little sign that says; *By crossing this threshold you accept rights and duties as guests of this house.* And what's the first thing you did as guests in my house? You killed another one of my guests."

"We didn't know," the Faerie pleaded.

Boy Scout wanted to smile, but he kept his face smooth as he leaned down next to the Red Cap's ear and whispered, "I didn't know what I was getting into when I cleaned up the graffiti in a skate park."

Boy Scout shoved the spike into the faerie's eye. He didn't bother talking to the others as he repeated this process.

After killing the last Red Cap, Cendrine asked, "Is that what I think it is?"

She tossed something at Boy Scout. He caught the green leather journal without thinking. Looking down, he saw the Celtic cross tooled into the cover. Two leather cords held it closed.

It was his, or it had been a long time ago.

He hadn't seen it since well before he'd gotten out of Faerie. He untied the leather chords. In the years since he'd held it last, the spine had loosened. It flopped open, and he barely managed to keep from dropping it. Still, a silver chain with a pair of dog tags and a white-gold wedding ring set with a sapphire fell to the floor, and a white card fluttered down after it. He recognized the ring, and the snap-crackle-pop of a breaking neck echoed up from his memories.

"Yeah." Boy Scout really wanted to shoot up. Not to forget. He couldn't forget, no matter how much he wanted to. The drugs just made it so that he didn't care that he remembered. "It's what you think it is."

If Cendrine said anything else, Boy Scout didn't hear her. He picked up the chain. The dog tags were his, not the ones he expected. Maybe that meant the last person he'd known to have that ring might still be alive.

Cendrine cleared her throat.

Boy Scout blinked, pushing memories and regrets away as best he could. Cendrine had picked up the white 3x5 card and now held it out to him between two fingers. He took it. Someone had written one sentence in flowing script onto the card.

Boy Scout who Lies, your friends need you. — Tommy

"Who is Tommy?" Cendrine asked, looking at the card from over Boy Scout's shoulder.

"An old friend. One of my oldest," Boy Scout shook his head. "But it can't be from Tommy." *Could it?* "The handwriting is wrong."

Granted, he hadn't seen Tommy's handwriting since they'd been fifteen years old; however, this handwriting wasn't anything like Tommy's had been. First off, whoever had written the card used a mix between standard print and cursive. Tommy almost always tried to write as close to Courier New font as possible, explaining to those who asked that it made him feel like a journalist. Boy Scout took in the nine words, trying to gain some sense of the author's identity; he noticed that the e's tilted slightly right and the crosses of the t's curved upward on the left. He got the feeling the writer was used to quick and precise movements with the fingers and wrists.

He opened the book. His own handwriting stared at him with the heading of *DAY ZERO* at the top of the first page. He flipped through the pages, passing the parts he'd written. Those days had sucked enough the first time, he didn't have any desire to relive them. About halfway through the journal, which was where Boy Scout had left off and given the book to someone else, the handwriting changed to a neat, precise cursive. Mary's first words in his old journal stared up at him.

MARY'S TRANSITION
(And my only post from this name.)

Boy Scout is gone. He and Wish went off with the princess this morning. I don't have a lot of time. Presto and Snow Shade say I need a new name since I'm taking over as platoon bard. Can we even be called a platoon anymore? I guess that's really up to the LT and Cuban to figure out. I'm just here to carry the personals and record all the shit storms we're probably going to have to weather as we try and make it back overdale. Gotta go for now. We're renaming me. I wonder if I'll feel any different.

Boy Scout stopped reading. He wasn't sure if he was ready to know what happened to the others. Would he ever be ready? Probably not.

He flipped through the rest of Mary's portion of the journal. Not all of it was in her handwriting, but Boy Scout didn't stop to examine it...until he came to a page that had been dog-eared. The handwriting on that page was his, though he couldn't ever remember writing those words down. Hating himself for his curiosity, Boy Scout read the next two pages in the journal

WISDOM I LEARNED FROM MY MOTHER'S BOOKS:

"The heart of wisdom is tolerance." — *Steven Erikson*
"Just because you're paranoid doesn't mean there isn't an invisible demon waiting to eat your face." — *Jim Butcher*
"It's like everyone tells a story about themselves inside their own head. Always. All the time. That story makes you what you are. We build ourselves out of that story." — *Patrick Rothfuss*
"Duty is heavy as a mountain, death as light as a feather." — *Robert Jordan*
"Evil is relative. You can't hang a sign on it. You can't touch it or taste it or cut it with a sword. Evil depends on where you are standing, pointing your index finger." — *Glen Cook*
"There are other worlds than these." — *Stephen King*

I didn't get most of this stuff until much later, and by then, it was too late.

MY FIRST TASTE OF REAL MAGIC

Tommy Knight, Phil Bailey, and I stood at the edge of the four-foot-high chain-link fence that served as the border between the place where you could skate your heart out, and the place where moms and dads with little kids in tow would scream at you if you did anything more than skate a straight line, without tricks, to the sidewalk. Our boards leaned against our legs, and we leaned against the fence. Thick, gray clouds had come in off the ocean.

"Whadya think, Max?" Phil asked. "Reckon it's safe to go in?"

I took another look at the graffiti. It was weird, containing only three colors: black, white, and gray. The artist had blended them together in a way that made it hard to tell where one color stopped and the other began. Its shape was also hard to grasp. At first I thought it was an oval, then a circle, then an oblong, blob-shaped thing. Yeah, it was weird, but it was cool.

34

We skated hard. Despite our protective gear, helmets, gloves, and knee and shoulder pads, I could feel the bruises forming all over my body from my falls. I'd be sore the next day, but that didn't matter, I'd be back tomorrow and every day after that for all of Christmas vacation. The park was officially closed on Christmas, but it didn't matter. Christmas was the one day a year McPherson took off so we could sneak in once we all opened our presents. At least one of us would get a new board, and we'd have to break it in.

We all sat at the top of the highest ramp, our legs dangling over the edge. Each breath we exhaled came out as a stream of mist. Sometimes we pinched our thumbs and index fingers together as we inhaled and blew our breath out through pursed lips, just like Tommy's older brother does it while straddling his motorcycle.

"Good day," Phil said.

"Best day ever," Tommy said.

We all nodded. It had been. It was a good sign of things to come during the vacation.

"I got to get back," I said. "My dad's going to help me with a new story."

"Cool," Phil said. "I can't wait to read it."

Phil and I got up.

"You coming?" Phil asked Tommy.

"Na," he said. "I'm going to go a couple more times before I head in."

That wasn't unusual. Tommy lived right across the street, so he got to hang out a little later than we did. We gave each other high fives all around.

As Phil and I left, I glanced at the graffiti. It looked bigger, and I thought I saw a hint of red mixed in with the white, gray, and black. The hairs on my arm stood on end, which had nothing to do with the evening chill. I thought about heading back for Tommy, but decided that it would be okay. McPherson was there; always watching to make sure nobody broke the rules.

We never saw Tommy again. At the skate park the next day, the graffiti was bigger, and there was this big bloodstain. Later, one of the newspapers mentioned that the blood stain matched Tommy's blood type. He disappeared – I refused to believe he was dead – two years, down to the very day, after my mother left Dad and me alone.

THREE DIFFERENT FUNERALS

That was a hard month. I lost:

One of my two best friends
All my fish because I was so depressed I didn't feed them for a week.

My first girlfriend because I ignored her longer than the fish.

I also started dreaming about this amazing girl with fiery hair. She's showed up during my REM sleep at least once a week, every week, until the war broke out.

Boy Scout looked at the card again.

Tommy.

He hadn't thought about Tommy in years. Odd that with everything Boy Scout couldn't forget, he hadn't thought about Tommy for all those years.

"So, what do you want to do?" Cendrine asked.

Boy Scout looked up at her. "What do you mean?"

She kicked the broken syringe.

Boy Scout licked his lips. He was really thirsty. He took in the carnage around him, gaze settling on the girl, her head twisted around at an impossible angle. Her lifeless eyes stared back at him, accusing him, just the way his best friend had looked six years earlier. He turned away, trying to keep his stomach from emptying at the thought of what he'd done with that girl. Her corpse represented the depths to which he'd allowed himself to fall.

God, I really want to shoot up.

It wasn't a physical need. The potion that sobered him up also cured his body's dependency on the drug. Boy Scout just didn't want to care again. He shot up, smoked weed, and drank himself puking drunk so that he didn't care that he couldn't forget.

Boy Scout glanced over at the crate where another loose floorboard containing at least a week's worth of forgetfulness. He went over to it and moved the floorboard aside.

"Great," Cendrine said as Boy Scout pulled out his hidden stash of drugs. "That's your solution."

"Stop acting like you know everything about me." Boy Scout tossed the drugs to the other side of the room. "Burn that."

Next, he brought out the plain black journal with a black gel pen clipped to the back cover. He'd gotten hold of both just after he'd gotten out of Faerie, just in case. He hadn't brought himself to use either.

"You're going to write?" Cendrine asked.

He nodded.

"Anything to do in the mean time? Or do you want me to just hang out?"

Boy Scout sat against a wall, took the pen, clicked the top, and set the tip against the first page.

"Collect the weapons," he replied.

"Which?"

"All of them." He paused, mouth hanging open as he considered a moment. "Yup. All. I have a feeling we're going to need them."

"That sounds foreboding," Cendrine said. "Seem to be falling back into your talents pretty quickly."

"Hasn't anything to do with talents or powers or anything like that." He gestured to indicate the corpses lying around the room. "Just my critical thinking skills at work."

Cendrine nodded. "You going to be alright in here?"

"You mean alone?"

She nodded again.

"As in, you think someone or something else might come after me?"

She shrugged.

"I'm good with letting whatever six Red Caps have for back up just come and get me. That's the safer and less painful option."

"Alright."

"Now," Boy Scout said, "shut up and let me write."

Taking a deep breath, Boy Scout forced himself to meet the dead girl's eyes. His sides clenched, and again his stomach threatened vomit. He clenched his teeth and forced his body under control as he waited for that tingle at the back of his head to come. It took a long time. While he waited, he tuned out everything in the world but the girl. When it came, and at last it did, the pen started moving across the page, first in his handwriting, but as he continued scribbling words on the page, the script changed to the handwriting of a dead girl, telling at least part of her story.

Cendrine stepped over the enforcer from Sunshine's brute squad and walked down the stairs to the next floor.

She recognized Bruno, having met him twice before. The second time was when she'd come to convince Sunshine and his brutes that trying to sell out Boy Scout was not in their best interest. Bruno had been good, not just big and strong, but quick and smart. He was the kind of guy who kept his wits in a fight, even when things turned against him. He stayed patient, always looking for a way to turn things around. But...he was only human, and no matter how clever he was, he wasn't a match for one Red Cap, let alone six. He was just as dead as the little harlot who'd slipped into the apartment and started all this trouble, though Bruno hadn't died from a broken neck. A wide gash stretched across his neck from where the Powries had slit him open and drenched their caps. It would be a miracle if anyone in this building was still alive.

The thought of six Red Caps working together sent a shiver through Cendrine's body. To her, fear was cold, complete, and utter lack of warmth. Not like the cold of a winter's day or an ice cube. No, it was the cold of the void, the cold that doesn't so much eat heat as it dissipates any warmth into the vast lack of existence. This soul-numbing chill came not from Oberon sending these Red Caps after a bard who hadn't practiced his gifts in years, but rather from him sending the Red Caps to *fetch* that bard. The King of Faerie had a plan for the bard and feared his power enough to send this kind of a force.

She stopped halfway between floors, a threshold between here and there within the building. This was the perfect place from which to search the building, and she should have thought of it sooner. It seemed that the bard wasn't the only one whose paranoia had grown lax in the years of waiting and waiting and nothing coming from that waiting. With that thought, Cendrine understood. What did the fey care of a year, or even a decade? Oberon could outwait them all. But still, in wanting the bard for something, the Faerie King couldn't wait too long, human lives being so fragile in their brevity.

Cocking her head to the side, Cendrine listened to the heat in the building. Bodies cooled on every floor. The bard was the only living thing in the building, or at least, the only living *mortal* thing. She couldn't hear any unnaturally cold spots, nor any cracks or corners with a lack of any temperature at all. That was something at least. It meant that Oberon probably didn't know about the tattoo, the enchantments bound within it, and all the strangenesses the boyscout bard had worked upon her with his talents and gifts before giving them up, well, before giving them up until just now.

She didn't know what to think about him writing again.

At the thought of him writing, her hand went to her pocket where she'd slipped the battered leather journal. That book held so many pieces and secrets to her past.

Cendrine drew the journal from her pocket and opened to the first page.

DAY ZERO

I'm calling this "Day Zero," because the platoon I've been assigned to is supposedly shipping out tomorrow. We probably will, but sometimes shit just happens. Whatever day we actually ship out on will be day one. My own personal version of D-Day. Stomach is already churning at the thought. That's me: Big Damn Hero (To quote one of Mom's favorite shows.)

Got my dog tags today. No name. Just my rank, religion, blood type, AB positive in my case, and my serial number. Faeries can use any personal information about you to do nasty things to your mind and your body. That means no real names underhill. Code names or nicknames only. Usually Platoon Sergeants give soldiers nicknames in boot/basic. I've never been through basic training, so I have no idea how that's going to work for me. Hope I don't get something lame.

Cendrine closed the journal.

Regardless of the answers it held, she couldn't afford to lose herself within its pages. She didn't even consider crossing over to the underhill to find a pocket where she might read the whole journal while mere moments passed here in the overdale. She flipped through the pages. Handwriting filled over half the pages. Cendrine sighed and slid the journal back into her pocket. Best not to seek answers she was not completely prepared for. Reading the journal would almost certainly answer some questions she'd always had, but it even more certainly would raise more questions. She couldn't be sure she'd have the patience to wait for an answer, and even if she could find the patience, those questions would distract her and cloud her judgment. She'd just keep this key to her past and unlock the door and step through when she had more time. For now, she'd wait and see what path the bard took from here, making sure to keep him alive to fill in whatever holes the journal didn't.

Right now, she needed to perform the ridiculous ritual to get into the secret alcove where the bard had hidden the duffle bag with his weapons.

She walked one and a half flights of stairs to the door leading out to the roof.

"Macbeth," Cendrine said. "Oops...I mean The Scottish Play."

Having said that, and with one of the empty apartments in the building having been converted to a theater, the old curse must be observed.

Cendrine opened the door and stepped outside in the chill Bay Area morning. She faced west, her back to the rising sun, and took a deep breath. Thankfully, no one would see her jump through these ridiculous hoops. This was probably part of the bard's master plan; not only was the ritual overly complex, performing it was so embarrassing most fey wouldn't be able to bring themselves to complete it.

"Macbeth, Macbeth, Macbeth," Cendrine said.

Then, she turned three times widdershins, spit over her left shoulder, and said, "God damn me to hell for a fool." Taking a deep breath to stall, she made sure she remembered the three lines before continuing. "Angels and ministers of grace defend us...If we shadows have offended...Fair thoughts and happy hours attend on you."

Having completed the ritual, she faced the door again and knocked, hoping she'd gotten everything right.

The door opened.

Now, down three flights of stairs. Seven steps into the third flight, she reached into the metal box embedded in the wall, the box that used to hold a fire extinguisher, and pulled out a ratty hand broom. She continued her journey downward. Four steps from the bottom of that flight of stairs, she bent down and began sweeping the third step.

"I am sent with broom before," she recited from *A Midsummer Night's Dream*, "to sweep the dust behind the door."

The top of that step vanished.

Cendrine reached into the empty space inside that stair and pulled out an olive-green duffle bag. It was heavier than she expected.

Hopefully, they could set everything right. She did not want to have to go through that idiocy ever again.

THE TROJAN HORSE

Writing is a socially acceptable form of schizophrenia.
— E.L. Doctorow

The scariest moment is always just before you start.
— On Writing, Stephen King

Her name is… Her name is…

I can't remember. Her corpse is lying there, lifeless eyes judging me because I can't remember her gawddamn name. What a shitfuck I turned out to be.

Damn. Hate this part…man I hate it so much. This is the hardest it's ever been, even harder than when I didn't even know what I was doing. I'm really missing when I didn't know what I was doing, back when the words of other people's stories just flowed from my mind, through my pen, and down onto the paper. Funny thing about mastering some skill or talent: when you're just starting out and don't know enough to be self-conscious, you jump right in with gusto, without worrying about how "hard" it's supposed to be; then the better you get at it, the more you worry about getting it "right." Fuck but I want this shit to be easy again. Hell…probably would be if I hadn't spent the last few years since I got out of Faerie avoiding anything resembling writing, reading, stories, and/or any form of artistic medium like the proverbial fucking plague.

Clichés in my writing for the fucking win…I can just imagine Professor Matthiason's eyes rolling just before slapping the table with his notebook. How many times do we have to go over familiar language in our writing? Well, sir, it's all I've got now…Besides, when was that last time you used your writing to shape the course of two worlds and had to live with that? So, take your nuggets of Creative Writing wisdom and fuck the hell off. I'm not…

wait…

there we go… First problem solved.

too focused on myself…gotta get out of myself…away from how those eyes are making me feel.

Before I try and jump into her, I need to get the extraneous crap out of my head. Man, oh man, I want to just give up, put the pen down, and get the fuck out of Dodge. Only…only…that won't really help anything in the long run, and when it comes down to the nitty and gritty, the six Powrie corpses lying around me means I have to find out how Oberon managed to track me down,

41

otherwise, he'll just do it again, and again, and again, ad nauseam, until something kills me or I manage to set things straight. Shoulda known my past would catch up with me, considering who I am, what I've done, what she has done, and that we never really settled things, not in any meaningful way. So, now I've decided to step up and be a man...well, that's what I'm telling myself anyway. Not sure I can handle more self-truth than that right now.

So, now I come back to the girl. She's all of a sudden the only trail I have back to how and why Oberon wants to draw me back into matters of the fey. She's the first step on my path to answers. I've seen her before, not just last night. But last night is as good a place as any to start. Start with that and work my way backward. She came with the drugs. That meant she was one of Sunshine's girls. I remember seeing her before, when Sunshine and I first started our business relationship. She was cleaner back then. Back then she didn't make house calls, or any kind of calls at all. Back then, she was Sunshine's Virgin.

"This is Christina," Sunshine said through his pearly white, overly wide smile. The introduction came with the dripping sleaze of a man showing off a human possession. "Don't be shy, Christina. Go say hello to my friend, Boy Scout."

"Boy Scout's your name?" the young lady asked.

"As good a name as any," the guy replied.

Christina walked across the room.

"Hello, Mister Boy Scout," she said with a sultriness to her voice that she didn't quite own. She and Sunshine were still working on that. He claimed that faeries he had to deal with were especially susceptible to virgins who dripped of sensuality and sexuality.

Christina stood on her tiptoes and kissed Boy Scout's cheek. She couldn't help but smile just a little bit when he blushed. That would make Sunshine happy. He might even give her a treat.

Having completed her mission, Christina walked back to her place next to Sunshine.

Something in that resonates when it's written, hums with the power of truth.

Christina walked...

No, not quite...

Christina walking...

No...something still not right there...

Christina walks...walked...getting there...

Christina walker

THERE

Christina Walker. Names have power that resonates in the world around them. They drop clues all over the place for those who understand what to look, listen, and feel for.

So, now that you've introduced yourself properly, Miss Christina Walker, please tell the readers a little more about yourself...

...myself...

Well, my life was pretty boring up until I was thirteen when I ran away from home after the Faerie War ended. The last thing I wanted to do was wallow away the best years of my life in boring-ass Cool, California. If ever someplace didn't live up to its name, Cool was that town...though I hear Paradise, California gives it a run for the money. Nothing cool ever happened in Cool. But out there, in the world beyond the lameness of my hometown, people were having adventures. Normal girls like me were marrying lords and princes from both Faerie courts, getting rich, famous, even a few of them signing to reality TV deals. Living a life I could. None of them were nearly as pretty or smart as me. So, I ran away to San Francisco, what better place to meet the Faerie prince of my dreams than a city with one of the last open gates to Faerie?

But I can sense that you don't care about that, and I don't really want to talk about how sad and pathetic it was for me after I got here. Long and short of it, I was in bad shape. Sunshine found me, cleaned me up, fed me, and treated me like a queen for a year and a half, until an even cuter model came along to be his virgin. Me, well, he told me that I owed him, and that I could work off my debt. Somewhere about six months later, I paid off my debt once and for all...which wasn't even an hour ago.

Oh, you don't want to come that far forward? Don't want to hear that you travel in circles that trade a fifteen-year-old girl's life as a business favor? Didn't seem to matter much to you last night while we were doped out of our minds doing the horizontal tango like you wouldn't believe. What's that? Too much truth for you right now? Sucks to be you, doesn't it? You got sober and can move on. I just got dead.

Fine...we'll hit the rewind button and go back to last night.

I stood outside the door as Bruno, Sunshine's enforcer, rapped his huge knuckles against the door in a complex rhythm — two long, two short, a medium, a short, a long, a medium, and then I lost track. I was too fascinated by the glowing runes and sigils that appeared on the doorframe as he knocked. Bruno repeated the pattern. This time, Bruno knocked on the doorframe, tapping a specific symbol with each knock. Once he finished, Bruno moved back up the hall, leaving me alone.

A series of locks rattled on the other side of the door. I swallowed. This wasn't the first time Sunshine had sent me as a customer appreciation gift, but it was the first time I did get sent to Boy Scout. I remember him being nice to me the few times we met, back when he still came to pick up at Sunshine's office. I'd also never been sent to someone with instructions to not get turned away, no matter what happened. If I got in and answered the door in the morning, Sunshine promised I'd never be a customer appreciation bonus again. Joke's on me for that one.

The door opened less than an inch, and a bloodshot eye looked out at me.
"Where's Bruno?"
"I'm here," Bruno replied.
"Let me see you."
Bruno came back down the hall. He gently, but firmly, moved me aside.
"Here."
Then Bruno put me back and stepped away.

I smiled as sweetly as I could. I figured Boy Scout would go for the all-American-girl more than he would the under-aged-sex-slut thing most of Sunshine's other clients went for.

"Sunshine sent me with this week's delivery." I opened my trench coat. I had the drugs taped between my tits. "I'm your preferred customer bonus."

Boy Scout's eye wandered over my body. Man, he was hard to read. I wished I could see his whole face and get a better read. He opened the door a little further. I took a small step forward. He held out his hand, stopping me.

"Just the drugs," he said.

Not going to happen. This was my way out. Fuck your morals, Mister Boy Scout. You're going to let me in. I'm going to be here all night. Let the heroin help you deal with it after I'm gone.

I tilted my head forward, chewed on the right corner of my lower lip, and half closed my eyes. That expression never failed to sway a man.

"Please let me in," I whispered, almost pleading. "If I don't spend at least an hour in here, Bruno will wonder, and then Sunshine will wonder, and then I'm going to get punished."

The real desperation in my voice surprised me. Not because Sunshine would punish me. I'd been punished before. I just hadn't realized how much I needed this to work so I'd never have to turn a trick again. Lol... There's that joke on me.

"Put this in your hand," Boy Scout said, holding out a railroad spike.
I took it.
"Put it against your forehead."
I did.

"Put it against your navel."

I did.

"Now your nipple."

I did.

This wasn't the weirdest fetish thing I'd done, but then I realized this wasn't about Boy Scout getting off on some strange power game. He was testing to see if I was a faerie.

He seemed satisfied, because he opened the door wider, and said, "Come in."

"Thank you," I said.

After crossing the threshold, I went right to the bed, or at least the ragged futon that passed for a bed. It wasn't the worst place I'd fucked one of Sunshine's customers, and if fucking this guy meant I'd never have to fuck another guy again, I'd fuck him on a bed of shattered glass and rusty nails.

"Oooo, candlelight," I said, as I untaped the drugs from my chest and the kit from my ass. "How romantic."

"It's not for you," Boy Scout said, closing the door and putting thirteen intricate locks back into place. "You make it go out and I'm sending you back to Sunshine."

"No problem," I said. "Leave the candle alone. Got it."

Those locks would be a problem. I'd have to get him to an epic high in order to get those unlocked before morning. Dope him up, screw his brains out, dope him up again, and he should be so far gone that I could get done what I needed done.

DEAD WEIGHT: The Tombs

A KNIGHT WITHOUT ARMOR
IN A SAVAGE LAND

The noir hero is a knight in blood caked armor.
He's dirty and he does his best to deny the fact that he's a hero the whole time.
— Frank Miller

Typically, the hero of the fairy tale achieves a domestic, microcosmic triumph,
and the hero of myth a world-historical, macrocosmic triumph. Whereas the
former – the youngest or despised child who becomes the master of extraordinary
powers – prevails over his personal oppressors, the latter brings back from his
adventure the means for the regeneration of his society as a whole.
— Joseph Campbell

Boy Scout threw the journal across the room.

He took a deep breath, held it, then let it out over the course of ten heartbeats.

It didn't help.

The gel pen joined the journal a moment later.

He'd let Christina Walker into his apartment because… well… road to Hell and intentions and all that. Sunshine came across as friendly, all smiles, a real jes' folks kind of guy – well, most of the time, anyway. When Sunshine got mad or felt like someone had crossed him, he made the Spanish Inquisition look like, well, Boy Scout didn't know what it looked like, as he'd never been dumb enough to cross the gangster, but word on the street was that it involved long hours of severe pain followed by a drop off one of the bridges. Boy Scout couldn't let that happen to Christina, not that. She'd looked at him with those sad, tired eyes, and stuck that lip out with just the right quiver. He just wanted to shoot up, go to sleep, and let her out in the morning. Well, the shooting up part was easy. He tried to stop her from kissing him, her hands wandering over his body…only, the drugs kicked in and broke down his morals and inhibitions, as drugs do, and he was kissing her back…and then his hands started roaming, too.

47

Tears welled up in the inner corners of his eyes as his gut churned. Shame. Disgust. Horror. Abstract words that couldn't begin to describe how he felt bounced around his head while he wanted to slap himself, claw his eyes out, and then slam enough junk into his arm to kill an elephant.

"Real fucking boy scout I turned out to be," he muttered through clenched teeth.

He looked out the window. The day grew even lighter beyond the window. How easy would it be to jump out again, but ignore the fire escape this time? He had his pants on, so he wouldn't have to worry about the embarrassment.

"Figure out our next move?" Cendrine asked from the doorway.

She had the duffle bag slung over one shoulder. He saw the green leather of his old war journal poking up out of the side pocket of her cargo pants.

"You read it?" he asked.

"Not yet," she replied.

"How tempted were you?"

"Not very."

She walked over to the journal he'd flung across the room, dropping the duffle bag about halfway through the journey. Kneeling, she reached down and picked up the journal.

"Aahh," Boy Scout started, but his voice caught in his throat when she fixed him with a cold, stony gaze.

Cendrine's eyes scanned back and forth across the page. Like always, her face bore no emotion.

How did she feel about it? Did it matter? Even if she hated him for it – of course that presupposed that she didn't hate him before – Boy Scout was pretty sure she wouldn't walk away from him. Hell, all things considered, she probably couldn't even if she wanted to.

It didn't take long for Cendrine to finish reading. She gazed at him over the journal in which he'd written Christina Walker's story.

"Well?" Cendrine asked.

"Well, what?" Boy Scout countered.

"You never answered my question."

"Ah, which question was that?"

She shook her head. "Have you figured out what our next move is?"

"Our?"

She sighed. "Jesus fucking Christ. Can you pretty fucking please with a cherry, whipped cream, and chocolate fucking sprinkles suck it up and get over your self-pity party? Oberon sent a team of Red Caps to fetch you and bring you back. Team. Of. Red Caps. Have you considered that he sent them not because he thought that one Red Cap might not be able to bring you back, but maybe, just maybe, because someone else is after you, and the king of fucking Faerie felt they could protect you while they delivered you to him?"

"Actually," Boy Scout said, "no, I hadn't considered that. Been a while since I've used my critical thinking skills in any capacity outside of finding stuff to keep me well out of screaming distance of my right mind. It didn't help that one of them threatened to bleed me out. But it makes sense once I recall that fey, especially Powries, are prone to exaggeration. I just can't imagine what or who would be coming after me besides Oberon."

"So?" Cendrine asked. "What do we do now?"

"Stick with the original plan," Boy Scout said. "See what Sunshine knows. I can't imagine the Powries setting this up. It's not in their nature."

"True," Cendrine said. "So, you think Sunshine has something to do with this?"

"Yeah, I do," Boy Scout said. "He's the starting point. Then follow that trail wherever until we figure out what's going on and why it's going on now. Yeah. That feels right."

"What does?"

Boy Scout gave her a slight smile. "Why now? That's the big question. With all the wonky-wibbly-wobbly effect that the Faerie, especially the sidhe, have on time, why is Oberon suddenly interested in me now? Not while I was still in Faerie where and when it would be easier to grab me. Not next week, or next year, or next decade. Now. That's the key to it all. Why specifically now? We figure that out, and we can work at turning this toward our advantage."

Cendrine crossed her arms. "No more running?"

"Nope."

However, Boy Scout considered the other hideouts and safe houses he had secreted around the world. He could run. He might even find enough drugs to hide from himself, but that was never long enough. The problem was, despite Boy Scout's best efforts, Oberon had found him. That meant that, no matter how far Boy

Scout ran, the King of Faerie could find him again. The longer it took, the more people would get hurt, people like Christina Walker.

"Why now?"

"Because she," Boy Scout pointed at Christina's body, "and that," he pointed at his old war journal poking up out of Cendrine's pocket, "reminded me why people call me Boy Scout."

He walked over to the window. The sun had risen completely over the Oakland hills over in the east bay. Helicopter rotors echoed faintly in the air, patrolling from the base in Alameda making sure nothing big and scary snuck through the gateway from underhill during the night. Garbage and wrecked cars filled the streets. A few of the shops on the first floors of the buildings were opening for the day, but most remained either boarded up or empty husks.

"Come here," Boy Scout said.

Cendrine stepped up beside him.

"See that empty shop on the corner with the taxi cab driven through the front window?" Boy Scout asked.

"Yes."

"I used to put up with mediocre burritos there because the margaritas were so good. Two blocks down used to be a shop, Siegal's, where you could get honest-to-god custom zootsuits. I know that because I had a few friends really into swing dancing. I never got into it, too busy writing. Working on a story, I'd go and eat mediocre burritos and drink kick-ass margaritas. A few blocks up and over was my mom's favorite bookstore when I was a kid. Borderlands. She'd read them to me. Taught me a lot."

"Like that list in your journal?" Cendrine asked.

"Like that, but more," Boy Scout replied. "Way more. Her books probably saved my life more times than I want to count during the war. I miss her. I also miss the way San Francisco was when I was a kid. I just can't seem to keep from fucking it up."

Cendrine placed a hand on his shoulder, the first gesture of comfort or affection she'd shown him in a long time.

"It's not like all this is your fault," she said.

Boy Scout turned toward her, and spoke slowly, "All this," he waved out the window, "is my fault. All my fault. Just like her," he waved at Christina, "I had the best intentions, but...well...I fucked it up."

"You can't blame yourself for her," Cendrine said. "The Powries killed her."

50

Not knowing whether to laugh or cry, Boy Scout looked over at the broken syringe. "It would be so easy to go back to not caring again." Boy Scout licked his lips. "The trouble is that I do care. Even doped out so far from sanity a pair of seven league boots wouldn't get me back in, I care."

"So, now what?"

"Give me the journal," he replied, holding out his hand, "and the pen."

Cendrine reached down to his old war journal.

"No." He held up his hand. "You hold onto that. Anything happens to me, you should have that. Read it when you have time. If I'm still around, I'll answer any other questions as best I can."

Cendrine nodded and handed Boy Scout the other journal and the gel pen.

Boy Scout turned to the next blank page and wrote these words:

Trustworthy
Loyal
Helpful
Friendly
Courteous
Kind
Obedient
Cheerful
Thrifty
Brave
Clean
Reverent

"What's that?" Cendrine asked.

"The boy scout law," Boy Scout replied. "It's easy to forget our principles when wallowing in self-pity. Sometimes we need to take a minute and remind ourselves what's important."

"Alright then, you ready?"

"Soon as I finish getting dressed," Boy Scout replied, "and load up."

Even so far removed from the war and his time with the Marines, Boy Scout's mind and body fell into sync.

Within just a few minutes Boy Scout was dressed in black cargo pants, easier to move in than the blue jeans, a pair of worn but comfortable boots that made no sound and left no trace of his passing, and lastly, a gray T-shirt which canceled any and all kinetic energy that made contact with it. Then he put on his brown leather jacket, which was just a normal jacket, excepting completely mundane alterations of a custom holster on the right side and a *sgian dubh*, a short-bladed Scottish knife, hidden in each sleeve.

Once he finished lacing his boots, Boy Scout went to the duffle bag. He rubbed his hands together and licked his lips before kneeling down and unzipping it. With a deep breath and a sigh, he reached in and took out his Irish fighting dirk. He held it by the scabbard in both hands so that each end of the belt hung down. He hefted the weight of it. Physically, it was only a few pounds, but the lives he'd taken with it seemed to strain the muscles in his arms and shoulders. Even though Boy Scout knew that this was just a trick of his mind, the years had done nothing to distance him from his past. Despite his desire and prayers to never take it up again, he'd known this day would come, that he couldn't hide forever. Someday, someone underhill would want to make use of his talents.

"Well…shit," Boy Scout said, and belted the dirk around his waist so that he could draw it backhanded with his right hand or cross-draw it with his left. He let the weight of it settle onto his hips. "Yeah, this is all full of suckage."

Next, he put the rosary with interspaced silver and iron beads around his neck and slipped it under his shirt. Oddly, the rosary filled him more with relief than the expected dread. But then, the rosary wasn't meant to harm. More than likely, it would protect him and repel potential threats. After the rosary, he put on the chain with his own dog tags, though lighter than anything else he wore, they pulled his neck and shoulders downward with the memories that came with them. He didn't want to wear the tags, but you never know when those might come in handy.

Lastly, Boy Scout stared at the remaining item in the bag, a wooden gun case. After a few moments thought, he opened the gun case and picked up the weapon inside. He didn't know what it was made of, but it looked like a Glock made of glass. Anyone who looked closely at its insides would see all the mechanisms of a firearm, only clear – even the bullets in the magazine were clear. Without pausing to test the pistol's weight or balance, Boy Scout put it in the holster inside his jacket. He took the two spare magazines and slid them into his back pocket.

Standing, he faced Cendrine.

"Ready?" she asked.

Boy Scout opened his mouth, ready to spout a line from another movie his mother had loved, *I was born ready*, but he couldn't say it.

"No." Boy Scout shook his head. "Not anywhere close to being ready, but that doesn't mean a damned thing. It's gotta be done."

Cendrine nodded at him, and they left the apartment.

Boy Scout's apartment remained quiet for several minutes after Boy Scout and Cendrine left in their search for Sunshine.

Even though daylight now spilled through the windows, the closet remained dark with shadows, darker than perhaps it should have. Boy Scout hadn't bothered to reset the wards because he didn't ever expect to return here. That meant the closet remained open as a portal between worlds. The shadows deepened even more in the closet, not shrouding it in complete darkness, but near enough.

Two people stepped out.

The first was a woman in her mid to late twenties wearing an artist's smock that had probably been white years before the Faerie War, now covered in specks and splotches of paint. Her ruddy blond hair, shaved at the sides and also flecked with dried paint, was pulled back into a bun and held in place with a pair of paint brushes.

The other woman hid most of her features beneath a gray, hooded, long coat with only her lips, chin, and the ends of her twin platinum blond braids visible.

The cloaked woman waited by the closet door while the first went to the middle of the room and took a magnifying glass out of her smock's pocket, knelt down, and examined bits of broken glass.

"That's it," she said, putting the magnifying glass back in the pocket and bringing out a pair of tweezers and a plastic bag. She carefully picked up the pieces of broken glass that had Boy Scout's blood on them.

"Will it be enough?" the woman by the door asked in a whisper.

"Yes," the artist replied. "Enough for both a painting and a weapon."

"And you're certain this is the only way?" the whisperer asked.

"Yes." The artist stood and went back to the closet. "With everything else he's been through, seen, and knows, it's the only way he's going to commit to action one way or another. It doesn't matter which way he goes, but until he picks a side, both underhill and overdale are going to keep spinning out of control until it gets so bad that nobody will be able to fix things."

Having gotten what they came for, the two women stepped back into the closet. A few moments later, the deep shadows made way for the light pouring in from the windows.

Boy Scout stopped in midstride. His breath caught in his throat at seeing the barricade and soldiers in urban fatigues at the 16th street BART station. After calming down, Boy Scout thanked whatever subconscious impulse had made him decide to circle around rather than come straight down Mission to Sunshine's lair, where those Marines would have seen them from at least a block away. In his hurry to backtrack onto Capp, Boy Scout came close to knocking Cendrine over.

"Problem?" she asked, pushing him away.

"Only that Sunshine has relocated," Boy Scout replied.

Cendrine poked her head around the corner.

"The army men might have him," she said.

"Those are Marines, not army," Boy Scout said, "and they don't. Those barricades and fortifications are older than the last 24 hours. If the Marines had him, then I wouldn't have gotten a visit from Bruno and Christina last night."

"So what now?" Cendrine asked.

"Gotta figure out where Sunshine's new lair is."

"Lair? Really?"

"It's Sunshine's term for where he sets up shop. Though, he does do his best to make his place live up to the term."

Cendrine fixed Boy Scout with a glare that might set off a bonfire inside him if she wished it. "Are you actually defending that waste of human flesh?"

"No," Boy Scout replied. "I'm defending the justified use of language in an appropriate context." He sighed. "Why can't anything ever be easy?"

Cendrine opened her mouth. Boy Scout held up his hand.

"Don't say it. A man can dream that the universe will cut him a break now and then."

Cendrine snorted. "I hardly think karma is finished fucking with you yet."

Realizing that further banter would not only be pointless but also more embarrassing – damn but he was out of practice – Boy Scout headed back down Capp Street. Behind him, Cendrine said something, but Boy Scout waved her off.

Why would the Marines be setting up a fortified position so close to the gateway? For that matter, why a BART station? Considering the number of Unseelie fey that inhabited the underground tunnels, well, that just gave the Marines one more point to worry about defending.

Unless…

Boy Scout stopped. He closed his eyes and visualized the maps of the San Francisco Bay Area public transportation system, specifically BART and MUNI lines. He'd used both a lot before the war and the map of those multicolored routes had burned themselves into his mind's eye…especially those near a certain skate park. Then he put a few things together in his head, like the fey might actually be the ones to deal with the Marines underground rather than the other way around.

"Holy shit," Boy Scout said.

"What?" Cendrine asked.

He ignored her as he took off running down Capp Street, not even bothering to see if she followed.

A block and a half later, Boy Scout had to walk. Panting and wheezing, he'd maxed out his endurance. Brilliant plan to stay cooped up in his apartment, keeping his mind in a fog, hoping that two worlds would forget about him. Yeah, Dad sure did raise a bright one.

"Want to tell me what's going on?" Cendrine asked, as she came up next to him.

He waved her off, not because he didn't want to answer her, but because he couldn't form words without gasping. This remaining sliver of pride surprised him. Besides, he needed to keep what little breath he had for walking the next seven or so blocks.

They passed people and fey, fellow derelicts mostly. At one point, a gang of kids – all human, the oldest of them might have been the same age as Christina Walker – walked toward them. The two biggest of them puffed up and lifted their weapons. One had a baseball bat with iron nails driven through it. The other had a nail gun. Cendrine stepped over to a dying tree and ran her finger across its trunk like a strike-all match. The tree wasn't very big, maybe two feet taller than Boy Scout, and it had no leaves, but it went up like it had been soaked in napalm. The two biggest kids unpuffed, and the gang moved to the other side of the street.

As they went, one of the smaller girls kept looking at Cendrine.

"What?" Cendrine asked as the tree burned bedside her.

"Nice shirt," the girl said, pointing and flashing the smile all fanboys and fangirls share when they run into someone who loves the same thing they love. "I love those books."

Cendrine's face twitched, and then her face lit up with the same sort of smile. More of her humanity than Boy Scout had ever seen showed through her features.

"Thanks," Cendrine said. "I love 'em, too."

"Using the bet in book two has saved my life a couple times since I came to SF," the girl said.

"Just don't go trying how they won in book three," Cendrine said.

The girl's face stretched wide with shock. "I'm clever, not stupid."

"Good girl. Stay safe, and don't try too hard to be clever."

"See ya 'round," the girl said, waving. Then she jogged to catch up with the others.

"Maybe," Cendrine said.

As the gang of kids walked away, Cendrine blew out the tree with all the effort of a child blowing out a single candle on a cake.

She held up a hand in front of Boy Scout's face. "Not a word?"

"Didn't I get you those books?" he asked.

"Shut up," she said, and started walking again.

A few blocks later Boy Scout and Cendrine came across a fire team of four Marines. Boy Scout saw them too late to avoid them. They had the now-standard mix of gear for fighting both conventional and faerie threats. Boy Scout remembered how long it had taken him to get used to the sight of crossbows, swords, and axes alongside assault rifles and grenades. Without waiting to see if they'd approach and question what must be the strangest pair wandering around the Tombs, Boy Scout pulled his dog tags out of his shirt and rattled them in front of his face.

"Designation?" the lance corporal asked.

"Bard," Boy Scout replied.

The lance corporal opened his mouth, blinked, closed his mouth, blinked again, and then opened his mouth again. After all that, though, he wound up just asking, "Here?"

Boy Scout nodded. "T.Y.S. People overdale don't much like that I spontaneously write their secrets. Don't mean to, but I was underhill too long writing soldiers' stories to keep them remembered back here. Sometimes I can't control the when or where. Gets awkward."

"Sorry to hear that, sir," the lance corporal said, and saluted. "Thanks for your sacrifice."

Guilt and shame wrenched at Boy Scout's stomach as he returned the salute. The dog tags swung heavy in his hand and beat against his face.

Once the fire team moved on, Cendrine said, "T.Y.S?"

"Thousand year stare," Boy Scout replied, slipping the dog tags back under his shirt. "Term for bards whose power takes over them."

Cendrine fell into step beside Boy Scout as they resumed their journey. Last time he'd been out of the apartment, the troops stationed in San Francisco hadn't been patrolling the Tombs. It had been considered primarily Faerie territory, well, Faerie and those humans idiotic enough to sneak in.

"Those soldiers seemed to respect you," Cendrine said after half a block. "Maybe we could get some help from them."

"No." Boy Scout quickened his stride just a bit.

Cendrine matched his pace, and pressed further. "But, surely someone in their ranks might know something. You just have to ask the right people."

"No." He stopped and turned to face Cendrine. "Don't press this. You can call me to task on a great many things. You can berate my choices and throw the past in my face. This, I will not budge on. We are not involving the military. Period. End of discussion."

Without giving her time to respond, Boy Scout executed a text-book left flank and continued down the street. Cendrine didn't bring it up again. They walked in silence the rest of the way down Capp Street. When they reached 24th, Boy Scout peeked around the corner of the building, looking toward Mission Street. Just like at 16th Street, the Marines had turned the 24th BART station into another fortified position.

"Son of a bitch," Boy Scout said. "That's why."

"That's why what?" Cendrine asked.

"Oberon is sending goons for me now. The U.S. is getting ready to attack the gateway, and they aren't being very subtle about it. Whoever is calling the shots might think they are being really clever, but if I can figure it out, at least several dozen of the sidhe will work it out, too."

"Are you sure?"

He rolled his eyes, though made a point to not to do so until after he looked back to the BART station.

"Pretty sure."

For a moment Boy Scout considered dropping into Socrates mode, posing questions leading Cendrine to the answer on her own, but he remembered she hadn't grown up in San Francisco, learning, memorizing, the crisscrossing web of transportation lines and schedules. That lack of experience meant it was unfair of Boy Scout to expect her to comprehend the potential tactical and strategic value of controlling the BART and MUNI tunnels.

"They, that's the U.S. military, could have thousands of troops waiting in those tunnels, ready to pour out and strike at the biggest gateway between Faerie and our world. If they coordinate that with air support, they might have a shot at closing it."

"That could reignite the war," Cendrine said. "Do you really think they'd do that?"

"Americans don't take well to other people trying to grab our crap," Boy Scout replied, turning back to her, "especially our real estate. Should have expected this to happen. I bet they've spent the last few years working out new technology to more efficiently kill faeries. It's what we do in every war we've ever been in. And the fey are the only force to ever successfully encroach on sovereign U.S. soil. I can't imagine that sitting well with anyone high up in the military or the government."

"So what do we do about it?"

"We figure out where Sunshine is and we have a chat with him."

"That's still your priority?"

"Yup." He smiled a tight, humorless smile. "I'm tired of being other people's pawn. Hell, I'm tired of being bound by the bonds of Faerie itself. This is the Twenty-First Century, not ancient Ireland. Somehow, someway, I have to be able to break the shackles of the Old Laws and write some new ones."

As Boy Scout spoke those words, the very air about them became charged with the power of story. The air seemed to thin, making him feel lightheaded. His skin tingled in the way it did when someone had left the window to a room open and the faintest of drafts caressed the skin on the arms and the back of the neck.

He'd known that sensation only a few times before, when a bard became the embodiment of the ideal warrior poet. Cendrine wouldn't be able to feel it. She had too much Faerie blood to feel that power. Most humans couldn't either, especially in the Twenty-First Century, when humanity had forgotten the power of story. Boy Scout imagined it used to be different, that people used to seek these moments, these times when true story buzzed about the world, giving those people who reached out and took hold of the chance to create tales that lived for centuries and millennia beyond them, rather than the way that media for profit had diluted Warhol's fifteen minutes into flashes of sound bites, 140 characters, viewer rankings, and shareholder expectations. In its quest for instantaneous knowledge, it had killed its ability to have true heroes.

Boy Scout wondered if he could change that. Was such a thing possible? He held no illusions or delusions that he could be a hero. After everything he'd done and not done, he could live with that.

"Come on," Boy Scout said, turning on his heel and heading back down Capp Street. "Going to be a busy day."

"Where are we going?" Cendrine asked.

"Union Square," Boy Scout replied.

"The place where they make the music?"

"That's the place."

"Why would Sunshine be there?"

"He's probably not. He's probably still in the Tombs somewhere."

"Then why Union Square? Isn't that a bit out of our way?"

"Maybe. Maybe not. Depends on your point of view."

"I can't wait to hear this explanation."

"Not all stories happen in a linear narrative."

"That makes no bloody sense."

Boy Scout laughed and kept walking, leaving her to wonder.

The artist stared through the wide lens magnifying the blood caked on the shards of glass that had recently been a syringe. Two dozen paint tubes of reds and browns surrounded the objects of her attention.

"Well?" the other whispered from the chair next to the easel and canvas.

"Well what?" the artist asked.

"We're working on a limited timeline here," the whisper replied. "Shouldn't you get to the actual painting sometime soon?"

"I don't bitch and moan and kvetch about how you do your killing. Don't presume to tell me how to do my painting."

Still, she began selecting hues of paint to mix with the Writer's blood to use in her painting.

The sun shone high overhead as Boy Scout and Cendrine reached Market Street close to noon. Time had been unkind to the brick sidewalks of Market Street. Holes gaped here and there where bricks used to be. People – humans, faeries, and even a few half-bloods – filed up and down both sides of the street. Against the buildings, people had set up tables and pop-up tents to sell clothes, jewelry, charms, books, CDs, art, and more. It felt like a surreal acid-dropping sister of Telegraph Avenue in Berkeley before the war…before the Unseelie razed Berkeley to the ground in an attempt to purge a potential hotbed of bardic talents the U.S. could turn against them. The condition of the sidewalks and the foot traffic forced Boy Scout and Cendrine to keep glancing down to be sure of their footing then back to eye level to keep from bumping into anyone.

The crowds thinned as they came up on the Powell Street BART station.

"That's interesting," Boy Scout said.

"What?" Cendrine asked.

He pointed to the massive iron plates etched with silver runes riveted to the ground blocking off the underground entrances to both the BART and MUNI lines. He looked across the street. The same thing had happened to the entrance there as well.

"Looks pretty new," Cendrine said.

"Yep." Boy Scout nodded.

"Seems this fits in with your earlier assessment," Cendrine said. "A straightforward way to keep the riffraff out."

"Yep." He started off again.

"Why are we here?" Cendrine asked. "I'm still thinking this is a little out of the way if Sunshine is in the Tombs."

"Right," Boy Scout said. "But not all stories have a linear progression."

"Yeah, you mentioned that," Cendrine said. "Care to explain?"

"I just did." Boy Scout replied, pleased that for once, she was the one trying to keep up with him.

They continued down Market until Boy Scout heard the beginnings of music. The wind was right and carried the sounds a block earlier than he expected. So many instruments wove together in a chaotic cacophony that flowed in and out of being painful and sublime and brilliant and ear-wrenchingly bad. He turned right toward Union Square, and the noise grew. When they reached the corner of Powell and Geary, Union Square came into view, and nothing had changed. Musicians, both individuals and bands, filled Union Square proper. Dancers and performance artists filled the sidewalk surrounding the square. This close, when the musicians went out of sync with each other, the effect was almost painful.

Cendrine said something.

Boy Scout leaned closer to her. "What?"

"We're going in there?" Cendrine almost had to shout for Boy Scout to hear her.

Boy Scout nodded.

Before crossing the street, he went over to a girl sitting against a building. She was in her mid-twenties. Sunglasses hid her eyes, though the mop of unruly brown hair might have done that as well. She wore a mix of ragged fatigues and what might have been a fairly cool gypsy costume, once upon a time. She had a sign, black marker on cardboard, that read: *TYS burned me out. Can't sing. Voice gone. Please help. Have ear plugs. Used and unused.*

Boy Scout pulled his pen and the new journal out of his pocket and knelt down in front of her.

"Trade you a secret for two pairs of ear plugs," he said.

She looked him up and down. "Bullshit. You got no muse."

He pulled his dog tags out of his shirt and showed them to her. She slid the sunglasses down a bit to better read the tags. Boy Scout decided he liked the girl's deep green eyes. Pretty, despite the way they didn't quite focus on anything while trying to focus on everything. Her lips formed silent words as she read his number. She blinked a couple of times in rapid succession. Any bard with any talent would know that number.

"Uh, uh, uh," she stammered. Seems she got just as articulate as he did when life surprised her.

"Calm down," Boy Scout said. "No drama. No scene. No names...especially not here. I just want to trade a secret for two pairs of ear plugs. Deal?"

"Not just a secret." The girl swallowed. "I want a True Secret."

It wasn't a request or an offer; it was her price, straight up, take it or leave it.

Boy Scout drew in a deep breath and let it out slowly. He glanced around to see if anyone had heard her. No one seemed to have paid any attention to her. Perhaps this was the universe throwing him a bone. If so, he was grateful. Having that get around in this place was not any kind of attention he wanted.

"That's a big fat can of Lovecraftian nightmare worms. You sure you want to open that?"

Her eyes grew wide and she held her breath for about ten seconds while she licked her lips. The air around her seemed to thicken with the tension of her choice. Finally, she gave three nods in quick succession. She blinked, let out a heavy breath, and the tension around her faded.

The girl held out her right hand.

For a moment, Boy Scout thought about refusing. This girl couldn't be the only one selling ear plugs. He thought about the last girl he'd tried to help. Christina Walker's dead gaze stared at Boy Scout from within his mind's eye. He clenched his teeth and rubbed his hand over his face. When he looked again, the girl still had her hand out to him.

"Ah, hell," he said, wondering why it seemed impossible for him to say no to anyone even remotely resembling a damsel in distress.

Another face rose out of Boy Scout's past: high cheekbones, green eyes of creamy jade, and hair the color of a summer sunset. She would be why. Somehow, someway, if he helped enough damsels, it might make up for her.

Boy Scout took the girl's hand. They shook, once, twice, and three times – a bargain made.

Boy Scout looked back and up over his shoulder to Cendrine. She fidgeted from one foot to the other, eyes shifting back and forth, trying to keep her attention on as many of the passersby as she could.

"Need a heat mirage," Boy Scout said.

Cendrine stopped bouncing side to side and glared right at him.

"Really?" she asked, her tone flat and oddly cool. When Boy Scout nodded, she added, "You don't think that's going to be a little conspicuous?"

"Not as conspicuous as what I'm about to do," he replied.

"Oh, for fuck's sake," she snarled. "Really? I mean, *really*?"

"Yes, really. Trust me; you especially don't want to go in there," he gestured across the street to the musician-filled Union Square, "without ear plugs. Think about what's happening and the kind of people who are making it happen."

"Christ. Can't I just give her some money? Maybe some gold?"

"Too late," Boy Scout said. "Bargain's been struck."

Cendrine turned her back on Boy Scout and the former bardic girl. "I hate you so much."

A moment later, Boy Scout felt heat on his back, as if someone had placed a radiator behind him. When the temperature rose to an uncomfortable level, Boy Scout held out his hand. The girl placed her left hand onto his. Boy Scout stabbed her in the palm with his pen. She gasped. He tried to feel some semblance of sympathy for her, but she knew what she was getting into when she'd made the bargain. He pulled the pen from her skin, opened the journal to a random page in the middle, closed his eyes, and wrote.

He didn't write very long.

True Secrets, those devoid of gray area or room for interpretation, those containing the essence of a Truth about someone or something, were never complex. That's what made True Secrets so hard, and in many cases impossible, for people to figure out: when it came down to it, human beings can't handle simple, basic Truths; it leaves people too open, exposed, raw; that scares them, sometimes terrifies them to the point of insanity, and so people bury those Truths down beneath layers of half-lies, delusions, and good intentions; it's the only way the majority of humanity stays sane, and the reason why in the war so many bards took a giant red-rover-red-rover-send-the-bard-right-over headlong sprint over to bat-shit-crazy-town – too many of them learned too many True Secrets.

When he finished the single, brief sentence, Boy Scout fumbled with the journal a bit as he ripped the page out of it, folded it in half, and handed it to the girl. As soon as he did, the temperature around them cooled to Bay Area normal, which meant Boy Scout was going to be chilly for a while as the cool air caressed his sweat-soaked skin.

"The writing might be a bit sloppy," Boy Scout said, as the girl took hold, "but you'll be able to read it. Just wait until you get somewhere alone, quiet and alone. You know this, right?"

She was chewing her lower lip, and so didn't speak, but she nodded. With her other hand, the girl handed Boy Scout two pairs of brand new ear plugs still in their plastic seal.

"Thanks," Boy Scout said, then glanced at her hand, "Just because you have it, doesn't mean you have to read it."

She nodded. "I know."

Of course you do, Boy Scout thought to himself as he stood.

A trio of young men, probably not even twenty years old, had stopped and made a triangle around Boy Scout and Cendrine. Their clothes were thinning at the knees and frayed at the edges. Dirt blotched their skin in places almost like dark sores from some strange wasting sickness, and greasy hair stuck out at wild angles from their head. Two had scars on their faces, and one was missing a few fingers on both hands.

"What happened there?" the one in the middle said. "Musta been pretty important."

"I told you this would draw unwanted attention," Cendrine said.

People around them began making a wider and wider berth.

"It's always got to be something," Boy Scout couldn't help but sigh and roll his eyes. He addressed the spokesman. "I don't suppose that you'd be at all willing go against your natural tendencies to be a gaggle of twatwaffles and let this go? You know, between the lady," he gestured with his chin to Cendrine, "and me, it's just because it's not going to go well for you."

"I don't believe in faeries," the one on the left sneered at Cendrine, showing off two missing teeth and several others rotting.

"Can I?" Cendrine asked.

"No," Boy Scout said.

The toothless wonder muttered under his breath, "I don't believe in faeries, I don't, I don't. I don't believe in faeries, I don't, I don't."

Boy Scout shook his head in disbelief. He thought back to the question Master Sargent Cuban used to ask any time someone didn't live up to his expectation: *How is it possible that Saint Darwin has not asked you to join him yet?*

"Tell you what," Boy Scout said. "Let me give you an insight into your future, something that will get you out of trouble the next time you're about to step in it bigger than you ever have in your life? Deal?"

The three tough guys glanced back and forth, and even before the leader said, "Yeah, deal," Boy Scout knew he had them.

He took the pen and jammed it into the wound on his finger where he'd stabbed himself to call to Cendrine. Then he wrote a single sentence in the journal in his own blood. When he showed the words to them, their skin became a sickly pale with a hint of green as they read: *TRUE SECRET: Mess with any of the three of us and you will choke to death on your own vomit.*

"Will that do it, gentlemen?"

They said nothing. The bravado faded from them like a balloon with a slow leak as they slunk away down the street.

Once the three poster children for the Darwin awards had moved out of earshot, Cendrine leaned in right next to Boy Scout's ear, and asked, "You didn't really give them a True Secret did you?"

Boy Scout shook his head. "Nope."

"Funny," Cendrine said.

"Yup," he replied, and handed her a pair of the ear plugs.

He mashed up his ear plugs, shoved them into his ears, and marched across the street. Cendrine did the same.

"Why didn't you read it?" Cendrine asked.

"Read what?"

"Her True Secret."

"How do you know I—"

"I saw your face when you read that page in your journal," Cendrine interrupted, "and that wasn't even a True Secret. When you turned around, before you saw the idiot triplets, you looked melancholy, not terrified. Not hard to put things together when you pay attention."

"Right," Boy Scout said. "Seems like you just answered your own question."

Boy Scout smiled as they walked into Union Square. Every time he came here, he remembered the Plato quote he'd first heard in Philosophy 101: "Music is a moral law. It gives soul to the universe, wings to the mind, flight to the imagination, a charm to sadness, gaiety and life to everything. It is the essence of order and lends to all that is good and just and beautiful." Union Square embodied this. Dozens and dozens of musicians jammed, with no leader, no sheet music, and yet, over and over again, created beautiful harmonies together. Most times those harmonies lasted ten to thirty seconds, but sometimes longer, as much as a minute or more. The last record of everyone playing in harmony Boy Scout remembered was over five minutes. Proof that human creativity was the foundation of miracle.

Dancers – individuals, pairs, and groups – spun and wove and grooved around the musicians. Sometimes bumping into each other, but always polite and apologetic...well...at least they were when the music hadn't swept them so far away they stopped noticing.

A deep longing for junior high school settled in the pit of Boy Scout's stomach. Once he'd finished his regular homework and chores, he'd slip his headphones on and write, blasting music loud enough to shut out everything but words flowing out of his pen into the notebook. Computers were for schoolwork. For his stories, he loved doing it the old-fashioned way. He missed when the writing was just for him. Before his Eagle Scout project. Before College. Before his first journalism job, when he thought that somewhere, somehow, he had found a place mass media hadn't poisoned. The best times of his life had been back when it was him, the music, and the writing, writing whatever the hell he wanted.

Shaking off the pointless longing of nostalgia, Boy Scout kept scanning the crowd.

The song of Union Square merged. His mind put words to the melody, *beggar than a king*, words he'd heard earlier when he'd leapt outside his window to the fire escape. And then, the musicians wandered out of harmony, but it was enough to tell Boy Scout he'd come to the right place.

Heh, he thought. *Fire escape*. He'd never really considered how accurate that was until just now.

A group of dancers parted, and Boy Scout saw who he was looking for.

The man sat cross-legged, salt-and-pepper beard hanging out from underneath the mountain of rags that were his clothes. A battered metal cup sat on the ground just in front of him.

When Boy Scout walked over to the beggar, the man's deep dark eyes snapped open. The eyes weren't black, nor were they brown. They were dark, piercing down to Boy Scout's core, just as they had been the two other times they'd met.

Boy Scout dropped a coin into the cup. Even with the cacophony around them, the *clink* of the penny hitting the bottom echoed in Boy Scout's ear.

"Eh," the beggar said. "Wha…what's this?"

"A little something to help out," Boy Scout said. "Man sometimes gets cold, hungry, or thirsty."

Without taking his eyes away from Boy Scout, the beggar picked the cup up off the ground and shook it. The cup was silent. No coin rattled within.

"What the—?"

"Exactly kiddo," the beggar said. "What the…dot, dot, dot?" He sniffed and squinted at Boy Scout. "I remember you…Didn't you used to be smarter?"

"Not that we've ever seen," Cendrine muttered under her breath.

Boy Scout gaped up at her, not because she'd said it — he'd gotten used to her scathing opinion of him — but rather because he heard her over the music blaring around them.

"Shush, you," the beggar snapped, and threw the cup at her, catching her on the shoulder. "He was smart enough to keep you as his Martin."

"His what?" Cendrine asked.

The beggar shook his head. "Sorry, mixing artist with the metaphor, in sideways up. His wild card? Yeah…yeah." He laughed so hard he coughed. "What a stretch that one was. But yeah, he was smart enough to keep you as his wild card." He laughed again, then held up his hand. "No. Don't say nothing. S'bout me an' him now. You just hush, and not need to bat those gorgeous greens at me. Been a long time since a pretty face could sway me 'bout anything one way or t'other."

"What happened to the coin?" Boy Scout asked. "It was my last one and I'm desperate."

"You already played that game once before. Not that you can't play it twice. Or thrice, if luck smile down on you. Some people get that lucky when they down that far, but not many. Besides. You wasn't and still ain't that broke. You can't make something your last penny. It's gotta *BE* your last penny. You can cheat some of the Old Traditions. Not that one."

"I suppose you would know," Boy Scout said.

"You trying to be cutesy there, kiddo?" He picked up the cup again, which had somehow just gotten back in front of him. "Sayin' I'm old?"

"You? Old? Never!"

Boy Scout considered adding, *Just because you've been around since God was an altar boy doesn't mean you're old*, but he didn't think that would go over well. And...*and*...Boy Scout had the feeling that statement might be more true than not true.

"So that's it, then?" Boy Scout asked.

The beggar snorted. "Yeah. You *was* a hell of a lot smarter. Just going to give up like that?"

Boy Scout lifted his hands in frustration. "I've got no money."

"That all I care about? That alls I've become? No wonder the Unseelie kicked your asses so bad and why you can't get rid of em, Unseelie and Seelie alike. Even after the war, and magic, and all the wonder and terror, y'all...alls y'alls deserve what ya got...and what you're likely to get."

"How about I trade you a story for a story?"

"Naw...I don't feel like telling a story, and you don't want to hear one. Yeah, you were going to ask me to tell you a story about where to find someone, but that's not how it works. That's not a story, that's directions. Still, getting closer, close enough to help you out, because you won't get it fast enough, and I have elsewheres and elsewhens to be. So, I don't needs a story, but you needs the middle of one. You'll start it, but it'll be in the middle. When you think it's the end, and you'll write more, it won't be any, but the begin, a new beginning. But...but...you won't see or read that beginning. That's a living, live, real treasure hunt of a missing person's case older than the war itself, and someone tells it after you've gone to tell other stories. The end...yours, theirs, everyone's...will work out in the end. I suppose that's why they call them endings... In exchange for all that, I'll give you a map to what you seek."

With that, the raggedy man held out his hand.

Boy Scout stared at the beggar for a long time. The words had been English, and had pretty much been sentences, but still, he couldn't figure out what they meant.

The beggar sighed. "Write something. One page. Then you get the map to the best place to watch the Sunshine."

Boy Scout took the beggar's hand. They shook once, twice, three times – a bargain struck.

Boy Scout sat down and opened the newer journal.

"No," the beggar said. "Not that one. The other one. The scary one. The one that hurts you to even know it's still around. Open it and write me one page full of something on that first page."

Boy Scout licked his lips. "But that page already has writing on it."

"Does it?"

Boy Scout looked to Cendrine. "May I have it back, please?"

Cendrine glanced between Boy Scout and the beggar. She pursed her lips for a moment.

The beggar laughed. "Shoulda checked with the lady before striking such a bargain. You used to be better at this."

"Please, Cendrine?" Boy Scout asked.

Cendrine pulled the war journal out of her peacock feather coat and handed it to Boy Scout.

He opened it.

The first page was blank.

He flipped the page…

…and saw the familiar words in his familiar handwriting: *I'm calling this "Day Zero" because the platoon I've been assigned to is supposedly shipping out tomorrow. That will be day one. Kind of like our version of D-Day.*

He flipped back to the black front page.

"Fucking faerie magic," he muttered under his breath.

"Watch the tone, kiddo," the beggar said, "and the sentiment. Even though I had nothing to do with that page in that book, I know you was lipping off to me. I'm as human as you are."

"I seriously doubt that," Boy Scout said.

"Doubt all you want. Doesn't matter much none to me."

"Fine," Boy Scout said. "What do you want me to write?"

"Whatever you need to, only, write as if you were young again. Lose yourself in the joy of it, like when you still loved it."

Boy Scout took a deep breath, put pen to paper, and closed his eyes. What to write about…What…to…write…about…

Somewhere close by, someone sang, "A knight without armor in a savage land."

He opened his eyes. The pen was already flying across the page, leaving words in its wake.

We shouldn't need armor... *Morgan's words came echoing back to me when the troll bouncer stood up and flexed its talons at me. It might have gnashed its teeth, but I wasn't about to give it the satisfaction of looking up at it.*

When it figured out that I wasn't going to look up, the troll bent down and got up close and personal.

"We don't like yer kind 'round here," ten feet of gnarled, red-and-black-checkered-flannel-wearing troll snarled in my face.

Great, I thought, as the heat and stench of its breath burned my nostrils and I choked down bile, of all the trolls in Arcadia, I had to get one that embraced Deliverance as its paradigm for existence.

"We just need to go in and have a look around." Morgan stepped up next to me. "What you like or don't like, doesn't have anything to do with it."

The troll's head swiveled away from me. I sucked in a breath of sweet, contaminant-free air.

"What about you, Roland?" Morgan asked. "Do you care if big, dumb, and inbred likes our kind around here?"

"Look," I said, "we don't want any trouble, but there's a faerie inside who has greatly offended the Duke of Avalon."

"Well, ain't dat sweet."

The troll's head swiveled back to me. I kept my feet planted in place rather than step out of the blast radius of its breath.

"I give less crap than a goblin's black ass." I blinked for a second at that visual, but then shrugged it off trying to wrap my mind around the metaphor. Better to not try and fathom the inner workings of the troll's thought process. "I'd turn away Oberon hisself, iffin he came here. So any changeling *fetch dog can piss the hell off."*

Typical response from the Unseelie slums. Avalon is one of the nicer cities in Arcadia, but like everything in Arcadia, some parts have to balance, and since Avalon is primarily a Seelie city, it means Unseelie neighborhoods get pretty white-trash-ghettolicious to compensate.

"Don't make this harder than it has to be," Morgan said.

The warning to be civil surprised me. Morgan likes beating up big and scary Unseelie brutes, the bigger and scarier, the better.

"Go bother someone else, changeling," *again the word came as a curse. "You ain't gettin' in."*

"You expect to stop me?" Morgan asked. "Pixies bigger and stronger than you have tried to stop me and failed."

The troll snarled and reached for Morgan. Morgan dropped to her knees, forcing the troll to lean further over to grab her. Its hand barely touched her shoulder when Morgan dropped, braced against the ground, and kicked the troll where its foot met its leg. I pulled my pistol crossbow. Morgan rolled out of the way to avoid the toppling behemoth. The troll rolled over, and as it got to its knees, I had the quarrel an inch away from its nose.

The troll froze, staring cross-eyed at the iron-tipped point.

"Now that I have your attention," I said, "will you kindly open the door? If you don't, I'll be on my way. I'm sure my patron would be more than happy to let me close the bar. Permanently."

The troll swallowed. Most faeries, no matter which court they've sworn to, hate any form of the word permanent when it comes from a paladin.

The woman with the blond braids and the gray long coat looked at the painting as the artist's brush flew back and forth between the canvas and palette.

"Is that really how you're painting it?" came a whispered question.

The artist stopped working, the tip of her brush a centimeter from the canvas and dripping with paint.

"Yes," the artist replied.

"That uniform is ridiculous," the disgust dripped from her quiet words. "And a disposable razor…Really?"

"Get over yourself," the artist said, and continued painting.

Boy Scout turned the page and touched the pen to paper so he could continue writing. It didn't surprise him in the least when he found it blank.

"Stop," a voice said as a hand closed over his, keeping him from writing on. "I said a single page."

Boy Scout started, "But—"

"It is not the time to finish this story," the beggar said. "It is only time that you know it exists. You will know the whole and the truth of this tale before your story ends."

Boy Scout withdrew his pen from his battered and worn war journal, flipped back a page and skimmed over the words he'd just written. He flipped to the dog-eared page, and read the entry in his handwriting, the one that he'd never written, about the last time he saw Tommy. Memories of his childhood, playing *DnD* with Phil, Tommy, and some other friends: Tommy would always play a paladin, because it was the closest thing to his last name.

"Holy shit," Boy Scout said, and followed it up with, "and fuck you, hindsight."

"Now," the beggar said, "as a bargain fairly made, here is a map to the man you wish to speak with."

The beggar handed Boy Scout a small, thin black electronic device.

"That's not a map," Cendrine said.

"Yeah, it is," Boy Scout said. He looked at the beggar. "GPS? From you?"

The beggar shrugged, picked up his metal cup, stood up, and vanished into the crowd.

"That may be the oddest exchange I've ever witnessed," Cendrine said. "Who was that?"

"You'd rather not know," Boy Scout replied.

He held his breath as he turned on the GPS. After the beggar had left, it occurred to Boy Scout that he hadn't included making the map readable as part of the bargain. The beggar didn't seem the sort to mince up the wording of a bargain like that…but when dealing with ephemeral beings at the heart of legends that spanned across multiple realities, one could never take anything at face value. The GPS turned on. Had it not been charged, it would have been inconvenient, but not terrible. With power restored to most of the city by a motley group of enterprising Luchorpáns and other industrious faeries, they could have found someplace to charge it.

Cendrine shook his shoulder.

"What?" Boy Scout said.

"I asked, why don't I want to know and how can you be sure?" Cendrine asked, steam rising from her hair.

Boy Scout smiled patiently at her and shook his head.

"What?" Her face tightened, and she crossed her arms.

Life mirroring art, Boy Scout thought as passages from his mother's books came bubbling up from the recesses of his memory.

So few hours ago, she'd seemed to be the stronger of the two, *had* been the stronger. Nothing had changed for Cendrine. She remained as she'd been since stepping out of his closet. He, on the other hand, had become more the man he'd been when trekking through the wilds of Faerie, the questing hero.

"What?" Cendrine demanded.

"We are the embodiment of our choices," Boy Scout said.

"If you say so," Cendrine said. "Who was that man?"

Boy Scout slid the GPS into his pocket and placed his hands on her shoulders. The warmth of her flowed into his palms as if he was holding a pair of steaming mugs of tea. He looked her right in the eye and did his best not to flinch from the candle flames she had in place of pupils.

"I tell you honestly, because I care for you. As cheesy and sappy as it is, I love you, do not ask after that one or seek him out."

"But—"

"Please, Cendrine," Boy Scout said. "I know caution and prudence are not natural to fire, but please listen to me on this. I've given you plenty of reasons to ignore my council, which is why I don't give it, but this is different."

Cendrine gazed back at him, the flames in her eyes dancing as she studied him. She grew warmer, almost painful to Boy Scout's touch. Still, he did not let her go. After a few moments, she shrugged out of his grip.

"Alright," she said. "I won't look for him, but can't you at least—"

"No, Cendrine," Boy Scout said. "You *know* about the danger of names. Let it go. You do *not* want his attention. Look at what having it did to my life."

She opened her mouth to retort; Boy Scout knew the expression, and he raised an eyebrow. She closed her mouth and nodded.

Boy Scout let go of her and pulled the GPS out of his pocket. It had a saved address. It was right on the Bay, directly opposite the gate to Faerie at the 24th Street BART station – not to mention right by Warm Water Cove Park and Pier 80, perfect for landing and staging areas right off the Bay.

"What the fuck is going on?" Boy Scout asked to the universe in general, not actually expecting a response.

"Where is Sunshine?" Cendrine asked.

Boy Scout showed her the GPS.

"What the fuck *is* going on?" Cendrine asked Boy Scout. He could tell she actually did want an answer.

"Whatever it is," Boy Scout replied, "it's big, and not nearly as straightforward as it looks. If we hoof, we should be able to get this done before too late in the evening. I don't want to be out in the Tombs after dark if we can help it."

LINES IN THE SAND

The only rules that really matter are these: what a man can do and what a man can't do.
<u>Pirates of the Caribbean</u> – Jack Sparrow

No law can be sacred to me but that of my nature.
Good and bad are but names very readily transferable to that or this;
the only right is what is after my constitution, the only wrong what is against it.
<u>Self-Reliance</u> – Ralph Waldo Emerson

The artist waited at the edge of Warm Water Cove Park. She leaned against a lamppost with a painting tucked under her arm. Around her, the shadows grew long with the sun hidden on the far side of San Francisco. To the east, lights from the military base at Alameda shone from across the bay. Somewhere among the deepening shadows, the artist's quiet friend waited, just in case of a double cross.

After a few minutes, the man who commissioned the work approached her. He seemed somewhere in his fifties or sixties, and while he wore civilian clothes, his trimmed haircut and crisply pressed clothes told the astute observer that they could place decent money that he was ex-military. A cigar stuck out of the left side of his mouth.

"Is that it?" the man said, indicating with his chin the painting under her arm.

She nodded. "You don't have much time."

"You're sure he's coming?"

She reached into her pocket and pulled out the sketch she'd drawn of a Boy Scout. He stood in a room as he looked out a window facing a sun. A clock on the wall behind the Boy Scout had one hand and only four times: Dawn, noon, dusk, and midnight. The hand had almost come in line with dusk.

"I got bored waiting," she said. "He'll be there soon."

"Are you sure it's accurate?" the man asked.

"Everything I do nowadays is accurate," the artist said. "Everything he writes is accurate, and he hasn't even really been practicing the last few years. Then again, he hasn't had to."

She handed the man the painting.

"Thank you," he said.

"Don't thank me, yet," the artist replied. "Just make sure he doesn't see it. It's got to be in the room with him."

The man looked at the painting and shook his head. "He looks ridiculous in that uniform. I should've left him with his original name."

"No." She spoke in a somber tone. "He's going to live up to whatever name he is known by. If you hadn't renamed him, he would have lived up to the first one you gave him, and then where would we be?"

"Hard to tell," the man said.

"No it's not," the artist countered. "We'd be fucked." The man blinked in surprise. Why did everyone expect her to be the prim lady? "And we'd be fucked, up shit creek and screw the paddle; we wouldn't even have a goddamn boat. That's where we'd be. As it is, we're still up that creek, just not one hundred percent fucked yet, and at least we have a boat. That right there," she pointed at the painting, "might just be the paddle we need. Best get it to where it can do some good."

The man with his high-and-tight haircut peered at the artist for a few moments with an unwavering, unblinking gaze. She imagined he'd been a drill sergeant at one point, and thus, was probably used to people bigger, stronger, and meaner than she looked backing down from that stare. The thing he didn't take into account was that those bigger, stronger, and meaner people hadn't looked into the truth of the universe, painted so many True Secrets about the past, present, and future that they had the Thousand Year Stare crash down onto their mind, and then painted their way back out. In essence, the universe had taken its best shot at the artist and she'd said, "Fuck you," and gotten on with what needed doing. This man could stare all he wanted.

Finally, when she did not flinch, blink, or look away, the man nodded, executed a textbook about-face, and walked away.

A few moments later, the girl with the braids and the gray long coat came up next to the artist. The girl had a painting tucked underneath her arm, the painting that the artist had created using the Writer's blood.

"Ready?" the artist asked.

"Yes," came the quiet reply. "How much does that one know?"

"He thinks this is about revenge," the artist said. "He has no idea that Oberon is involved, that the Powries went after the Writer, or that we have a deeper agenda."

"This is a desperate gamble we're making, and it's entirely likely that this is going to kill him before he can help us."

"If that happens, we'll just have to find the new champion and hope they have more character."

"Well, let's hope he lives," the artist said, "or it will be a hell of a long wait before a new champion is old enough to try this again."

"This place is a dump," Cendrine said.

"All of Sunshine's places look like dumps from the outside," Boy Scout replied. "Cuts down on the riffraff."

They had stopped a block and a half away from the compound so that Boy Scout could rest. His feet, knees, and hips ached; his throat burned. He was *not* going to let himself get this out of shape ever again, and this time he meant it.

"Let me know when you're ready," Cendrine said.

Boy Scout nodded. He just wished he could keep Christina Walker's face from flashing in his mind. Taking a few breaths to steady himself, he prepared to go into the nest of vipers. Before starting out, he took out his journal, the new one, stabbed himself in the finger...again...and wrote a sentence: *No matter how much they search me, they will not find the glass gun.*

He held out his finger to Cendrine and clenched his teeth together as she cauterized the wound.

"You're being very free with your blood today," she said.

"Let's go," Boy Scout said.

"You sure?" Cendrine asked, her tone stating clearly that she didn't believe him.

"Yeah," Boy Scout said, starting out toward Sunshine's compound. "Body will hurt for a few more days, and the other stuff that's wrong with me will last a whole lot longer."

As they got closer, Boy Scout saw that the place had once been a mechanic's shop.

Four massive brutes – Boy Scout decided he was going to call them, "the Brute Squad" – stood by the gate and watched him and Cendrine approach. The Brute Squad members all wore identical dark suits. Image was a big part of the reason why, in the wake of the Faerie war, Sunshine had risen higher and faster than other criminal tyrants seeking to prey on the desperate poor of San Francisco. Sunshine demanded that each of his men adopt the appearance of businessmen rather than strong-arm toughs.

"I'm here to see Sunshine," Boy Scout said.

"Been expecting you," one of the Brute Squad said. "You can go in. The lady stays out here with us."

"I'm not staying with you," Cendrine said. "I have standards about the company I keep."

"Take a walk then," the spokesman said. "Pier Eighty is right that way." He gestured with his thumb, as if trying to hitch a ride. "Walk or stay. Makes no difference to me. You just don't go inside."

"Really?" Cendrine's voice got low and husky.

Boy Scout suddenly flashed to a memory of Cendrine's mother. He started to sweat, which had nothing to do with the sudden wave of heat spreading out from Cendrine.

"Really," the spokesman said.

Before Boy Scout could intercede, Cendrine tossed a brown bundle onto the sidewalk just in front of the Brute Squad.

"What's that?" Boy Scout and the spokesman asked at the same time.

Boy Scout knew even before Cendrine spoke.

"Six Powrie caps. Red Caps." She waited for that to sink in, but the brutes looked at her, blinking with a lack of comprehension. "I took those six this morning."

She paused again. This time they started to get it. All four took a step away from the brown bundle.

"Six Red Caps, gentlemen. I killed them. That was how my day *started*. It hasn't really improved since. Do not fuck with me. I will snuff your pathetic mortal lives like candles on a birthday cake. Then, without moving from this spot, I will reduce the compound behind you to ash and slag. The man who pays you to protect him will be dead before he even thinks to turn on a fan. What's more important, following his orders today or all of you being alive tomorrow?"

During her speech, the tips Cendrine's hair had transformed into tiny candle flames. Steam rose from her. The sidewalk around her feet blackened and charred.

The Brute Squad tensed, hands inching toward their coats.

Boy Scout scanned the area, taking in all the glass windows in the surrounding buildings. For a brief second he really, *really* wanted the Brute Squad to throw down. He'd been holding in his rage over Christina Walker all day, letting it fester into a bubbling rot in the dark places of his soul along with all the other pointless deaths that had filled his life. These fucktards were the perfect foils for venting his rage.

The sound of synthesized music came from the spokesman's coat pocket. The brute answered the cell phone, listened for a few seconds, and said, "Yes, sir," before returning the phone to his pocket.

"Mister Sunshine would like to welcome both of you," the spokesman said.

With the muffled buzz of an electric motor, the large metal gate behind the Brute Squad slid open a few feet.

The Brute Squad parted, and Boy Scout and Cendrine walked between them and through the gate. Thankfully, Cendrine had cooled back down after picking up the bundle of Powrie hats.

"Could you really reduce this place to ash and slag, that quickly?" Boy Scout whispered.

"Yes," Cendrine said, "but I would have killed you and anyone else in the heat radius. Still working on directing heat to specific locations."

"Good to know," Boy Scout said.

A man who made the guys on the Brute Squad look like members of a high school mathlete team stepped into the doorframe, filling it. If he'd played sports back in high school, Boy Scout would put money on him being a star at neanderball, position: offensive throwback.

The massive mound of flesh looked Boy Scout over. He poked at the blade on Boy Scout's hip and chuckled. "Old School?"

"Iron," Boy Scout said.

"Fair enough," the offensive throwback grunted. "Give it over, and all your weapons."

"Hospitality means nothing here?" Boy Scout said.

"Safer than sorrier," the throwback said.

"I'm a bard," Boy Scout said. "I'd be a fool to start anything just when I'm getting used to using my talents again."

The offensive throwback shook all over and made a sound that might have been laughter. "People still fall for that shit?"

"Most still do," Boy Scout said. "You have to admit, it was a pretty good propaganda campaign."

"True that," the throwback said, getting himself under control. He held out his hand. "Weapons."

"Can't blame a guy for trying."

Boy Scout gave over the short sword and the knife in his left sleeve. The throwback searched him and snorted when he found the knife in Boy Scout's other sleeve. Boy Scout shrugged sheepishly.

"Don't even think about touching me," Cendrine said. "I'm not carrying. I don't need to carry."

"What'll you do if I frisk you anyway?" the uber-brute grunted.

"I'll boil the flesh off your hands down to the bone," Cendrine replied.

The throwback swallowed, but he didn't step aside.

"Let it go, big guy," Boy Scout said. "Sunshine has at least one mage in there that can go against her if it gets ugly. Believe me, I don't want it to get ugly."

"Fine." He moved out of their way. "Her funeral if she starts something. Enter as you will."

Cendrine leaned toward Boy Scout and whispered, "You can really start a fight and not have it affect your bardic talents?"

"Not in the least," Boy Scout replied. "The original bards weren't called warrior poets for nothing."

Crossing the threshold, they saw the main garage had been converted into a kind of recreation room, complete with two bars, a pool table, a foosball table, couches, and TVs with all the game consoles and electronic toys. The place even had power this close to the gateway to Faerie. The room was dim. A little light still filtered in from the high windows near the ceiling, but not much, and only a few lights were on. Boy Scout rolled his eyes at the lava lamps over by one of the bars.

The first people he noticed were the two soldiers by the bar. Boy Scout couldn't see any metal shining on their collars. Their presence was strange, but not completely out of the realm of possibility. Word on the street said that Sunshine catered to some of the military personnel, giving them cash in exchanged for weapons and gear which sold for high prices in San Francisco.

Next, Boy Scout noticed the young women lounging on couches and in piles of pillows. They wore silk and satin lingerie just skimpy enough to make the imagination start working its magic on the male hormones. Christina Walker's face flashed in his mind's eye. Thinking of Christina while seeing the almost-naked girls sent Boy Scout's mind to the previous night. His stomach churned as he blinked to clear the image from his head.

Men in immaculate suits sat and stood around the room, trying to look innocuous, but Boy Scout knew better. Any men that Sunshine chose to be at a meeting like this – Sunshine had to know this was coming after Bruno and Christina didn't come back this morning – were anything but innocuous.

A door opened somewhere to Boy Scout's left, and a voice called "Greetings, my bard."

Boy Scout glanced to his left, and his breathing slowed, but not in a calm, I'm-just-chilling-out way. This was his my-subconscious-is-trying-to-tell-me-something's-out-of-whack breathing.

Sunshine stood in the open doorway to his office. The crime boss was a handsome black man, hair dyed golden blond. A former heavyweight boxer still in decent shame, he filled out his tailored suit enough to be intimidating without trying. Probably more intimidating with his warm and friendly smile.

"I'm not your bard." Boy Scout said.

"Give it a rest." Boy Scout went back to scanning the room, trying to put together everything that didn't add up and doing his absolute best to maintain a perfect poker face. "Call me your bard ever again, and I'll write a story in my own blood about you becoming the Golden Gate Bridge Troll's bitch."

"Is there really a Golden Gate Bridge Troll?" Cendrine asked.

"Yup," Boy Scout said, still looking. "He likes dark meat." Boy Scout didn't know if that was true, but he did know that Sunshine was touchy about color. Boy Scout dropped into a bad southern drawl when he added, "And young and purdy like our host."

Not counting the Marines over by the bar, Boy Scout counted seven guys in suits. Glancing back over his shoulder, he saw that the offensive throwback wasn't around. That made Boy Scout more nervous, especially with seven…no…make that *eight* men. Seeing the bald top of some guy's head in a La-Z-Boy made Boy Scout breathe a little easier. Whoever it was sat at an angle that made him hard to make out at first.

"Do we really need—?" Sunshine started, his voice dripping with enough artificial sweetener to kill a diabetic.

"Yes." Boy Scout cut him off, shifting to the side to get a better look La-Z-Boy-guy. "We really need those kinds of threats."

After sidestepping about a meter, he could see the back of the man's head...and the smoke rising from the glowing tip of a cigar sticking out of the left side of his mouth...and Boy Scout felt as if he'd been dowsed in ice water. Breathing became a challenge. It didn't matter how long Boy Scout lived, or how addled his mind grew with age, he would never, ever forget the back of that head, bald or not, especially not with the tiny birthmark just behind the man's right ear.

"Now just a minute," Sunshine said, without the usual lower pitch in his voice when he got angry.

What the hell was going on, and how many players had a part in this game? Now the soldiers made sense, and the number of dudes in suits set his hackles up again.

"Holy shit," Boy Scout said.

He wasn't sure if he was talking about seeing the back of his old platoon sergeant's head or figuring out how scary the girls had suddenly become when he realized none of them were hanging on any of the men. That might have been plausible, if only one, two, or maybe even three girls had been in the room. The girls could have been with Sunshine, but not so with...Boy Scout did another quick head count...seven girls.

Boy Scout's self-preservation instincts kicked into overdrive. This might be cross-the-streams bad.

"Shut up, Sunshine," Boy Scout snapped preemptively, sensing the crime boss about to spout off again. "I need to take care of something first."

Boy Scout turned around in a slow circle. He touched the thumb and pinky of his right hand and the thumb and ring finger of his left. As he turned, he muttered, "*Bain míniú as an cacamais seo, a striapaigh,*" under his breath over and over. Cendrine gaped at him as if he were mad. The translation: *Figure this one out, bitches* from Irish.

"What's he doing?" Sunshine said. "He's not supposed to know magic."

"He's not doing anything," said one of the mages, one leaning against the pool table. He wore a suit with a purple tint. He had pale skin, too pale to be completely human. He looked in his late twenties, but as with Cendrine and others like them, true age was hard to tell. "That's not magic."

Boy Scout kept turning, taking everything in: Two Marines, the sergeant, Sunshine, Cendrine, seven guys that didn't fit the build of the typical tough guys Sunshine would have in a meeting like this, and seven smoking hot chicks that looked like they could fill the pages of Miss Teen Fredrick's catalogue. Removing the extraneous people from the equation – himself, Cendrine, Sunshine, and the two other Marines, because odds were, they were with Sergeant Cuban – left the seven men and seven women adding up to a shit ton of bad. He'd learned to fear patterns of threes, in this case the soldiers, and sevens, in this case the mages and witches waiting to hatch whatever scheme Sunshine had going.

Once he put all that together in his head, Boy Scout understood he had it right. He made one last tally: one nasty scheming crime boss, seven mages, seven witches, and three Marines with who knew what agenda. Time to push a little more power into his spell.

When he came around to pool-table-guy again, Boy Scout stopped, flicked his fingers out, and gave a final, firm, "*Bain míniú as an cacamais seo, a striapaigh.*" He took a deep breath and steadied himself by bringing his hands slowly to his chest and letting them settle to his sides. "Yeah. No magic." Boy Scout shrugged. "Depends on who teaches you the craft. I spent a lot of time with Oberon's daughter while I was on a hero's quest in Faerie. Oh, and that would be the *real* Oberon, *not* that Unseelie pretender." Boy Scout stabbed his finger in the air toward pool table guy. "Who'd you learn from?"

"You should have accepted the offer from Oberon's messenger." Changing the subject pretty much confirmed that the guy didn't know as much as he'd like people to think. He also fell into Boy Scout's trap. "It would have made everything less awkward."

And you die first, Boy Scout thought.

"Shit," Sunshine said, as the man sitting in the La-Z-Boy stood up to his full height of six foot three inches.

The years hadn't been kind. He had more wrinkles, and his hair, though still regulation cut, had retreated, seemingly conceding the battle for the top of his head. The man chewed the cigar at the same time he puffed on it, a feat Boy Scout still couldn't figure out. His presence filled the room, and even though he was just a normal guy without any magic or supernatural abilities at all, he still scared the shit out of Boy Scout.

"Seems like we're at cross-purposes, Mister Sunshine." He spoke in a soft, even tone with a hint of a southern drawl. Still, despite his calmness, or perhaps because of it, he somehow managed to let everyone in the room know that Sunshine was screwed. "I get the impression you have not been entirely forthright with me."

"I-I-I...can ex...explain," Sunshine said.

One thing Boy Scout had learned, probably the most important thing he'd learned from his mother's books, the ones Dad hated, was that if you shovel bullshit with all your soul behind the load of crap, people buy it like a precious commodity. Screw fireballs, charm spells, divination, and all that hocus-pocus-bibity-bobity-peanut-butter-sandwich-phenomenal-cosmic-power that mages, witches, and wizards prattled on about — well-timed bullshit was the strongest magic in the universe.

The old platoon sergeant held up his hand. The two Marines by the bar had subtly shifted stances, ready to move.

"I think you're done talking," Cuban said. "I hear you're still going by Boy Scout."

"That's right," Boy Scout replied. "I gotta say, I'm surprised to see you here...Sergeant Cuban."

Cuban flashed a quick, modest smile. This out-of-character gesture surprised Boy Scout even more.

"It's Warrant Officer, now," Cuban said.

"A promotion. Nice," Boy Scout said. He thought about it for a second, and asked. "Doesn't that come right from the President for some specialized skillset or expertise? What's yours?"

Boy Scout scanned the room, looking for anything that might be an arcane symbol of power.

Cuban's modesty vanished. "You."

"Me?"

"Yes," Cuban said. "When I finally made it back from underhill, I learned what you are. My association with you got the attention of the Joint Chiefs. They asked me to head up a small task force to bring you in to answer for your war crimes against humanity."

Boy Scout pressed his hands to the side of his head. "You've got to be shitting me."

In the far corners of his logical mind, he knew this day would come. Just like he knew everything really was his fault, his responsibility. Christina Walker was a microcosmic expression of Boy Scout's passage through the world, always screwing things up for innocent people no matter how good his intentions were. His emotional mind kept playing tricks to keep him sane: he could keep running and hiding, just like it wasn't really his fault, because he never had any idea what was going on.

"I was a kid trying to clean up a neighborhood park," Boy Scout said.

"This does not absolve you of the responsibility," Cuban said.

Boy Scout should have known better than to expect any sympathy from him.

"What's he talking about?" Cendrine asked.

Boy Scout shook his head.

"Are you going to tell them," Cuban asked, "or am I?"

"Fuck you," Boy Scout said. He turned to Cendrine, "Warrant Officer Cuban is here to take me into custody so I can stand trial for starting the Faerie War."

"What?" Cendrine asked in little more than a whisper.

"Wait," Sunshine said. "What?"

Boy Scout faced Sunshine.

"Surprised?" Boy Scout asked. "Didn't you ever wonder why I worked so hard to hide? Just because you're paranoid doesn't mean millions of people don't think you are the biggest fuck-head since Hitler. " Boy Scout turned to face the rest of the room again. "For that matter, it makes me wonder why your pet mages and witches didn't tell you that."

The seven men and seven women in the room, with their too perfect clothes, stiffened.

"How?" pool table guy asked.

"Oh, come on," Boy Scout said. "You can't believe that you were actually fooling anyone, can you?" He looked from Sunshine, to Cuban, to pool-table-guy. "So you've got a problem. Y'all want me for different stuff. Sunshine is kinda fucked, because I think he thought he'd let you guys duke it out and give me over to the winner, but now I've ratted him out. So what's it going to be guys, O-beron or the U.S.?"

"Hey," Cendrine cut in, speaking to pool-table-guy, "you work for Oberon?"

"Yeah," he sneered back at her. "I serve a real master."

"Good one," Cendrine said. "I serve no one." She tossed the bundle of former Red Cap caps on the pool table. "Go tell your *real* master that his precious little pets are dead."

The pale mage jerked back as if she'd tossed a bundle of serpents instead. The mages and witches began sliding along the walls.

And just like that, Cendrine set things in motion. Boy Scout didn't know whether to be proud of her or to pity her.

Boy Scout had to figure something out, some way to even the odds, or at least throw a little chaos into this. He didn't really care if he got out of this, not at this point. He just didn't want Cendrine to suffer for his folly.

He took a deep breath. This was one of those moments like other moments before this that would shape his destiny: wanting to clean up a park, enlisting to serve, shooting a gun on a plain of obsidian, and pushing a needle into his arm for the first time.

Boy Scout turned back to Cuban. The mages were still moving around the room. Sunshine was inching back toward his office. Boy Scout didn't want to think of the hardware he had back there, not to mention the means to call his Brute Squad into the mix, likely with the offensive throwback taking point.

"Why the hell are you here?" Boy Scout demanded. "This isn't like you."

The Sergeant reached down and picked up something from the La-Z-Boy. He held up a painting of a man in a Boy Scout uniform getting gunned down by a gun wielding cigar. Boy Scout recognized the artistic style: most recently because he'd taken the tour of her work in San Francisco just before going into hiding, but also long ago when he was working to become an Eagle Scout.

"I'm here because someone needs to make sure you don't make the same mistakes again," Cuban said.

"Wow." It was all Boy Scout could say. It looked like a fairly fresh painting, the paint still glistening. "Wow." He thought she'd been dead since well before the war ended.

Then Boy Scout understood the ramifications of him, the Writer, and her, the Artist, still alive and active. Even more, if Oberon knew that and got his hands on both of them at the same time, well,

Boy Scout shuddered to think about the terrible things Oberon could accomplish then.

Boy Scout whirled on Sunshine. "You better pray either you or I die in this room tonight, or you will never know another moment's peace for the rest of your life, and I *will not* allow you to die young."

"Fuck you, you lying sack of shit." Now Sunshine's tone lowered as he pulled a gun and pointed it at Boy Scout. "You're lucky Oberon wants you alive."

Now it was time for some truly dazzling bullshit magic.

"Fuck me?" Boy Scout screeched. "Fuck you!" He whirled on Cuban, pointing. "And fuck you!" Then he screamed at the mages and witches. "You can all go fuck yourselves in one giant circle jerk, which is what I'm going to make you do if I get out of here alive. I'm sick and goddamn tired of being everyone's scapegoat and pawn."

Boy Scout started pacing in a circle, waving his arms.

"I. Was. A. Fucking. Kid. Can any of you get that through your thick fucking skulls? I didn't know anything about Faerie, much less the games the Seelie and Unseelie play with mortals as their pawns."

Boy Scout faced Cuban. "You want to see justice done? You've got it. Take your shot."

He turned to pool-table-guy. "You want to snatch me up and take me to your master?" Boy Scout pointed a finger at the lead mage and glared down it like a gun sight. He swept his gaze over all the arcane practitioners in the room. "Bring it, bitches. I faced down Oberon's personal pet magic bitch boy during the war and left his mind leaking out his brain like tapioca. You got nothing."

Boy Scout turned back to Sunshine and smiled.

"You. Mister opportunist. You want to ever feel safe again? You better kill me now. I make it out of here, I don't even have to find you. I'm a bard. No. I'm *the* bard. Creator of legends. No matter where you go, no matter how completely you think you can hide, you will fail, and you will know the full weight of a bardic curse. You've got one shot, and only one. Better make it good. The problem is, if you kill me, Oberon won't be too happy, will he? Welcome to the sucktastic world of the Old Laws where all your options blow."

"Don't even think about harming him," pool-table-guy said. "Oberon wants the bard. Come peacefully and we'll spare the girl."

"Oh, really?" Cendrine asked.

The room grew warmer.

Everything seemed still, and now the whole room seemed to buzz with the energy of potential movement that came with the anticipation of combat.

Sunshine fired. Seems he was more scared of Boy Scout than of Oberon. That had to be a first.

The shot hit Boy Scout in the chest. Because of his enchanted T-shirt, it felt like someone poking him hard in the chest. Sunshine gaped at his gun as if the weapon had personally betrayed him. It wasn't too far from the expression a kid might give a toy gun that had the audacity to run out of batteries.

More shots rang out as Boy Scout drew his glass gun. Cuban fired at Sunshine, clipping the crime boss in the shoulder and sending him scurrying back into the office. The two Marines by the bar shot at the mages. Three of the mages and two witches opened fire with pistols, which was smart, and a little scary. Human magic didn't work like in fantasy books or roleplaying games. It was more subtle. Devastating, but subtle, and unfortunately for mages and witches in combat, not anywhere near as fast as a bullet. Mixing bullets and magic meant they could do some serious damage.

While the bullets flew, Cendrine rushed forward, her hair a halo of flames around her. Smoke rose from the scorch marks where her feet touched the floor. She grabbed the bottom of a couch, set it ablaze, and flipped it across the room. Two witches and two mages were so focused on shooting at the Marines, they didn't see the couch until it slammed into them, pinning them to the wall.

Unlike human magic, Faerie magic could be quick, flashy, and instantly deadly.

Two shots hit Boy Scout in the back. He ignored them. Only a head shot would take him out of the fight, and those were challenging for even the best marksmen in the middle of a fight. He trusted Cendrine to take care of extraneous gunmen while he dealt with the leader.

Boy Scout took aim on pool-table-guy. He had a crystalline wand out and was waving it over a half-full wine glass. Boy Scout smiled. Oh the irony.

On the other side of the room, the two Marines by the bar stopped shooting. Their mouths opened, and Boy Scout imagined they must be screaming. Their stomachs erupted like bloody claymore mines, sending blood and entrails across half the room. The mages must have spiked the drinks with something to create a sympathetic connection. After that, it was only a matter of time before the mage ruined your day.

Subtle, but vicious. Time to put an end to that shit.

When Boy Scout had the glass gun trained on pool-table-guy, he squeezed the trigger.

Every piece of glass in the room – the windows, the glasses, the bottles behind the bars, everything – shattered and flew at pool-table-guy. The broken pieces of mirror slashed at the mage's face. Moments later the rest of the glass, every shard and sliver, gathered in a whirlwind around the mage. His screams lasted about a second.

With pistol in hand, Cuban smoothly walked through the room. With each step, he took aim and fired, took aim and fired. With every shot, a mage's or witch's head snapped back, each dropping to the floor. Cuban was no mere marksman; target shooters could not maintain that level of calm in full combat. No, Cuban was a machine of war.

After four or five shots – between gunfire, roaring flames, and screams in this enclosed space, Boy Scout's ears rang too much for him to be sure, Cuban aimed at one of the witches. She rubbed a rabbit's foot in one hand, and tossed a shower of green stuff all around her. Boy Scout didn't have to jump far to take the leap of logic that those were four-leaf clovers. Even so many didn't surprise him. Some GMO company was probably making a fortune mass-producing them.

Boy Scout shouted to Cuban, tried to warn him, but the old Marine's ears were probably ringing louder than Boy Scout's. Cuban's next shot backfired. Boy Scout turned away as the cigar dropped from Cuban's mouth and blood sprayed out of the back of his head.

Cendrine waved toward that witch. The fire from the couch enveloped the girl, along with the two mages next to her.

Spinning on the ball of his foot, Boy Scout turned back to the office door, looking for Sunshine. The crime boss burst out of the office, toting an automatic shotgun. A weapon like that could ruin anyone's day, even if they were protected by a T-shirt.

Sunshine mouthed something. Probably something intimidating. Boy Scout didn't bother to try and decipher it. Sunshine was nothing more than a thug with a gun. Along with everything else, Boy Scout had been a warrior. As a warrior, he'd learned the hard way to just put the enemy down as efficiently as possible.

Boy Scout squeezed the trigger while Sunshine was still posturing.

The whirlwind of glass spun away from pool-table-boy, shaving off a mage's arm as he waved a wand at Cendrine before enveloping Sunshine.

With Sunshine neutralized, Boy Scout glanced around, looking for further threats. Everyone else except Cendrine and one cowering witch was dead.

Flames whipped around Cendrine about halfway between the floor and the ceiling. Blood poured from a gash on her forehead, and her jacket was missing a bunch of peacock feathers on the right shoulder, revealing a patch of mangled flesh.

All told, the whole fight had lasted less than a minute. If not for Cuban and the two Marines, Boy Scout knew Cendrine might not have survived and he'd be trussed up and carted off to Oberon.

Blinking and shaking his head, Boy Scout tried to get some semblance of hearing back. This wasn't over yet.

He turned to the front door. Just as he'd predicted, the Brute Squad, offensive throwback at the lead, burst in.

Boy Scout imagined what the scene must look like to them: the corpses, charred furniture, the whirlwind of glass, swirling flames, and Boy Scout and Cendrine standing at the center of the carnage.

"Who wants to die first?" Boy Scout couldn't hear himself, but felt the vibrations in his throat.

In what must have been a rare moment of clarity, the Brute Squad slowly backed away toward the door.

"You!" Boy Scout pointed the glass gun at the throwback. "Wait."

The throwback stopped and waited.

"Leave my blades," Boy Scout said, gesturing toward the pool table with his gun.

The throwback complied. Without any sudden movements, he placed the weapons on the pool table. The rest of the Brute Squad did not wait for him before clearing out.

Once Boy Scout and Cendrine were alone again, Boy Scout went over to Cuban.

The platoon sergeant – that's how Boy Scout would always think of him, no matter what rank he currently held – stared blankly at the ceiling. A good portion of the back of his head was missing. When Boy Scout reached down and closed Cuban's eyes, part of their first conversation came back to him, reaching through all the years and all the deaths, *Lies. That's what we'll call you, 'cause lies are all that reporters report.* His first military name, given when he joined First Platoon of Mike Company. Thinking of that made him remember the card in his war journal. He pulled the journal out of his pocket and took out the card.

Boy Scout who Lies, your friends need you. — Tommy

Seems he wasn't done playing the questing hero.

He felt a comforting hand on his shoulder. He looked up. Cendrine knelt next to him, one hand on his shoulder, the other hand offered him a golden whisky flask. The gash on her forehead was only a thin, pale scratch, and the injury on her shoulder looked like a bad rash.

After taking a healthy swig from the ancient whiskey, back from when it truly was the water of life, the ringing in his ears faded.

"You alright?" Cendrine asked.

Boy Scout shook his head. "Something isn't right, not adding up." he flipped the card from Tommy over and over in his fingers like a professional card shark. "I think this card means that some of my old platoon is still around. If that's true, then he's the man that could have pulled us together and taken a stand."

"Could that platoon really make a difference at this point?" Cendrine asked.

"Yes," Boy Scout replied. He happened to glance at the painting, the one from the artist. "That's it!"

"What?"

He pointed at the painting. "She's alive and painting. I had the idea that Oberon wanted us both, well, yeah, he wants us both, but so does the government. That's why the troops are massing. The U.S. wants to manipulate the ancient game between Seelie and Unseelie champions to close the gate."

"Holy shit," Cendrine said. "I think you're right. What do we do?"

Boy Scout held up Tommy's note. "We find my friends."

"Where do we start?" Cendrine asked.

"I'm going to search the office, see if I can find anything out."

"Alright," Cendrine said. "I'll keep you from being interrupted."

"But first, need to take care of a few things."

Boy Scout felt around Cuban's neck and wasn't surprised when he found a set of dog tags. He pulled them off Cuban's body and put them on. A familiar pressure settled on Boy Scout's shoulders. He searched through the fallen soldier's pockets and found a polished cigar cutter. That went into Boy Scout's jacket pocket.

He took Cuban's hand. "You were one of the best men I've ever known."

Of all the soldiers whose burdens he'd carried, Boy Scout could never have imagined this. He drew in a deep breath, and sang in the tradition of their time underhill during the war.

> Oh, all the comrades e'er I had,
> They're sorry for my going away,

Cendrine joined in.

> And all the sweethearts e'er I had,
> They'd wish me one more day to stay,
> But since it falls unto my lot,
> That I should rise and you should not,
> I gently rise and softly call,
> That I should go and you should not,
> Good night and joy be with you all."

The verse ended, Boy Scout knelt, holding Cuban's hand.

"Not your fault," Cendrine said.

"Maybe," Boy Scout replied. "Fault and blame don't matter. Dead is dead, and like so many others, my actions led to this."

With a sigh, Boy Scout released Cuban's hand, stood up, and headed for Sunshine's office. Beyond the open door, Boy Scout saw a table covered in newspapers, parchments, and books. That looked as good a place as any to start looking for anything that might point him in the right direction.

EPILOGUE: THE SECOND

Don't only practice your art, but force your way into its secrets...
— Ludwig van Beethoven

There is nothing to writing.
All you do is sit down at a typewriter and bleed.
— Ernest Hemingway

Max finished writing.

He closed the journal. It felt odd, knowing that he'd written his last story. At least now he knew what happened. He only wished he could stick around and help settle things.

"Wish," he said. "There's someone I miss. Ah, well. I won't miss anyone soon."

He scooped up the journal and a clean sheet of paper. That paper was the important part.

When he turned to go back into the front room, Max saw a painting peeking out from behind the open door. Even if he'd glanced that way coming in, the door would have blocked his view. He moved the door so he could get a better look at the painting. It showed a man in a Boy Scout uniform getting skewered with a disposable razor by some gray creature with wild blond braids. Attached to the canvas was a plastic bag with the remains of a syringe.

"Well, that's how they did it." Clever girl that artist was.

He couldn't help but laugh. It wasn't really that funny, he supposed, but then it was...or maybe it was just blood loss.

In the front room, Cendrine knelt over the body of one of the mages, paused in the act of going through his pockets.

The surviving witch still huddled in the far corner, though now a ring of fire about two feet high kept her trapped there. Max stared at the flames. He found even more beauty in them frozen in time than he did leaping about.

After a few moments, Max closed his eyes and shook his head. Free of the flame's lure, he went over to Cendrine and lay down. He didn't want to fall over when he put himself back into time. Part of him wanted to see how long he could keep going in this place between moments, but then nothing would get settled. He'd been a selfish prick far too long. Time to cowboy up.

Once he got relatively comfortable, Max dipped his finger in the hole in his chest. He touched it to the sheet of paper and wrote five letters.

S-T-A-R-T.

Pain blossomed in his chest, causing him to miss Cendrine's initial reaction at having him appear out of nowhere. By the time the white-hot pain faded from Max's vision and he could think clearly enough to make out words, he only heard Cendrine muttering, "Dad, please Dad, please Dad."

He coughed, but managed to get out, "Sssssssshhhhh."

"Oh, thank fuck," she said, and scrambled to get the flask to his lips.

"It's not going to be enough." Max coughed and shook his head. Save it for," cough, "someone it can help."

Blood and phlegm bubbled up when he laughed. He tried to spit it out before talking again, but couldn't get enough air or strength in his chest. The gooey mess wound up rolling down his cheek.

"If I'd known this would get you to call me *Dad*, I would have impaled myself a long time ago."

"We'll figure something out." Cendrine did her best to wipe the blood from his face. "Just hang on. Please? Dad, hang on."

Max shook his head. He held up the journal.

"Run," he begged. "They will know when I die." Cough. "They'll come here." Cough. "Read...read Tommy's story. Find him. Then find...and protect...the next champion."

Tears rolled down Cendrine's cheeks. Well, they made it about halfway down before boiling away to steam. Max felt nothing but cold. Yeah, that was a great sign.

He closed his eyes, ready for the darkness to take him.

She kissed his forehead. He felt the warmth of her lips there and smiled. That almost made dying worth it...almost.

Then he felt her breath next to his ear. She drew in a deep breath, and then sang him away.

Of all the money that e'er I had
I've spent it in good company
And all the harm that e'er I've done
Alas it was to none but me
And all I've done for want of wit
To memory now I can't recall
So fill to me the parting glass
Good night and joy be with you all.

Of all the comrades that e'er I had
They are sorry for my going away
And all the sweethearts that e'er I had
They would wish me one more day to stay
But since it falls unto my lot
That I should rise and you should not
I'll gently rise and I'll softly call
Good night and joy be with you all

A man may drink and not be drunk
A man may fight and not be slain
A man may court a pretty girl
And perhaps be welcomed back again
But since it has so ought to be
By a time to rise and a time to fall
Come fill to me the parting glass
Good night and joy be with you all
Good night and joy be with you all.

Max's smile grew as his body and mind faded away.

She sounded so much like her mother…her voice made it easy to go gentle into that good night.

An Excerpt from:
DEAD WEIGHT: Search and Destroy

THE TOUR:
A Second Prologue (of sorts)

"Come away, O human child!
To the waters and the wild
With a faery, hand in hand,
For the world's more full of weeping than you can understand."
— W.B. Yeats

"This concludes our regular tour," the slightly robotic voice spoke from the headphones Violet had received at the beginning of the tour.

Violet knew every speech of every display by heart, and sometimes recited the whole thing verbatim on her morning walk to high school. She collected anything she could find that showed the artist's work, hoping against hope that she would find something like the keyhole to light off the spark of bardic magic she knew she had inside of her.

When they returned to the artist house and entered the final room, Violet noticed some new paintings she hadn't seen on the tour before. A man in an immaculate suit reading a battered leather journal in a room with no doors. A platoon of Marines holding off a hoard of faeries, fighting on a plain of some smooth black substance, perhaps glass or obsidian. Some guy leaning over a table of books, scrolls, and papers getting stabbed in the back by a girl with platinum-blond braids wearing a black coat. A different girl, a red head, trapped in a cell with an old-fashioned typewriter, churning out page after page of writing. A young woman getting hit by an out-of-control driver, and a man in a uniform grieving, weeping on her coffin. A young man in a Marine uniform and old man dressed all in rags amidst something like those old Renaissance faires mom and dad used to tell her about, only the faire was filled with faerie

97

creatures instead of costumed performers. That young Marine was the same one who got stabbed in the back in the other picture.

"For the expanded tour," the voice in the headphones continued, "which allows you to look through the keyhole, please see information desk for the release form and appropriate donation rates." She'd been waiting for this part of the speech since she started the tour — no, since her parents had agreed to bring her here for her birthday. "Have a great day, and we hope to see you again."

Ever since the first time she'd come on the tour on a sixth grade field trip, Violet had wanted to look in the keyhole painting. She'd begged her parents to sign the release, and no matter how much pleaded, how many chores she promised to do, how many times she threatened to run away to one of the wild zones, they wouldn't sign for her. When they asked her what she wanted for her sixteenth birthday, and she told them and still nothing.

"You have a gift," her father had said while discussing her birthday over dinner. "I know you want to use it to help people, but right now, you're still a child. I know it doesn't feel like it, but you'll have to trust your mother and me to know what's best for you right now."

But they didn't know. They couldn't know.

Taking three deep breaths, Violet guesstimated the number of steps between her and her goal. It seemed about seven. She should have expected that. She'd knew about the Old Traditions. She understood the dangerous world she'd be diving into if this worked.

At the end of her third breath, Violet jumped over the velvet rope that kept tourists from the keyhole painting.

On the first step, Violet heard gasps of surprise, and Mother said, "What are you…"

On her second step, the guards called for her to stop.

Third step. Father shouted. "Miss Violet Craige! Get back here this instant!"

Four steps in, Mother's shriek rose above everything else.

More than half-way there.

One of the security guards reached for Violet.

She dodged with her fifth step, moving a bit diagonally as well as forward. The angle wasn't enough to keep the guard's fingers from tightening on the collar of her jacket. He yanked hard on the jacket. While planning this out in her mind, she figured at least one guard would get to her. She'd worn her baggiest jacket just in case. The jacket slid off her arms and shoulders as Violet's sixth step brought her back in line with her target.

More people called out behind her, some in surprise and some in anger. Still ignoring them, Violet, went right into her seventh step and put her eye right up to the keyhole.

Time … slowed … Violet blinked … in a prolonged moment … blackness shrouded her vision … words echoed in Violet's inner ears … bubbling up from the memories of times past … times spent hanging out with artists and dancers …

Time becomes fluid and mutable at the slightest touch of Faerie.

Her eyes opened…

She saw a skate park. Graffiti covered the concrete where people would normally be tricking their way across on their skateboards, impressing themselves and each other. Only, it wasn't normal graffiti tagging. The images were murals of dark buildings: Towers, castles, and fortresses. Each building trapped away somehow: chains, boards, and bricks kept windows and doors shut, moats and forests of thorns made certain that nobody within could escape. At one end of the skate park, a girl in her late teens worked with spray paint and brushes to finish another of these fortifications. At the other end of the concrete, a teenage boy, wearing a Boy Scout uniform and a few years younger than the artist, worked on hands and knees with cleaning supplies to scrub the artist's paint away from the concrete …

… Violet … blinked …

She saw a hill with green grass. Deep purple sky with gray-green clouds stretched across the horizon. Three people walked on the hill. The boy from the previous painting walked in the center. While he still wore the standard Boy Scout shirt, the rest of his clothes were a military uniform. He was also a few years older. Another soldier walked to his right. To his left was a girl, but not the girl from the skate park. This one wore a gray long coat with voluminous hood. Two braids, so blond they were almost white, hung out of the hood. In her left hand, she carried a straight razor big enough to …

… Violet … blinked …

The girl with the gray coat and the braids and the artist from the first painting stood over the Boy Scout. Again, he was few years older. He had a dark bloodstain on his chest and lay in a pool of blood. This time, rather than a still frame, the scene moved. Both girls looked at Violet. "It's your turn," they whispered …

… Violet … blinked …

Each of the previous scenes had become more and more realistic, making Violet feel more and more as if she wasn't looking at paintings as much as she was experiencing a series of moments. This time, when Violet opened her eyes, she wasn't looking at a painting, or even experiencing a moment that a painting depicted; instead, she somehow found herself within one of those moments.

She stood in a room, someone's small, personal library. It was a little larger than her parents' bedroom. Each wall was lined with bookshelves, from floor to ceiling, with the exception of the wooden door that looked like it belonged in a castle, three large windows that let in plenty of light, and the fireplace, which, at the moment, had no fire burning. The room was furnished with four push chairs, a table between the chairs, a stand with a chessboard, and a desk over by the fireplace. The table between the four chairs had a tray with a teapot and two tea cups.

The door opened.

Violet jumped, looked for a place to hide, and then, realizing how silly that would be, she stood up straight and tried to keep from holding her breath — a bad habit she had when she was nervous.

A man walked in. Violet first fixated on his cloths. He wore a billowy shirt with sleeves that hung to his knees, an orange wool vest, and plaid trousers, all of them patched, raggedy, and threadbare. He had a cloak that was more tatters than anything else wrapped around his shoulders. His hair and beard, mostly gray, were unkempt and wild as his cloths.

He smiled at Violet and gave a little bow.

"Happy birthday, young lady," the man said.

"How did you—"

"Hush," the man said. "Best if you don't any anything. The beginning of the conversation wouldn't be so bad, but any subject we might talk about, you and I, considering what you just chose to do, would very quickly tread on dangerous ground."

"Now hold on—"

"To what?"

"Wait, what?" Violet asked, confused. "What are you talking about?"

"You said, 'Now hold on,'" the man said. "Well…what do you want me to hold onto?"

Violet opened her mouth, and blinked a couple of times at the raggedy man. She ran her hand through her hair, wondering if he was being serious or not.

"I…" she said. "I don't want you to hold onto anything. I—"

"Then why bring it up?" He shook his head and waved his left hand at her. "Never mind. I don't want to know. Keep your cryptic bardic wisdom to yourself."

Violet opened her mouth, to ask a question. What that question was, she never found out. She'd had several on her mind, but didn't know which she was going to ask first. As she considered, the man pointed to one of the chairs.

"Sit," the man said. "Don't speak."

Violet sat in one of the chairs. She sank into the soft cushions and could imagine sitting here forever, reading all of the books this room had to offer. When she had settled into the chair, the man poured a cup of tea and set it in front of her.

"Look, it's bad enough they brought you here, considering who they are and who you're about to be. Then, oh, this gets rich, then they ask me to give you," he reached into one of his sleeves and pulled out a battered journal and thrust it into Violet's hands, "this. Like I wanted the responsibility of hanging onto that thing."

"And why would I want it?" Violet manged to get in while he paused for breath.

"Hush!" The raggedy man thumped her on the forehead with is middle finger. "Why is 'no talking' such a difficult concept to grasp? That's rhetorical by-the by. The last thing we need, is you prattling on about this, that, or the other thing before the mantle of faerie magic settles on you completely."

He stopped for breath again. Violet waited a second, then opened her mouth. She closed it again when the man raised his hand, wiggled his fingers, and glared at her forehead. Violet closed her mouth.

"Good," the man said. He tapped the journal. "Read. Read all of it. I must away. Shenanigans to get into, people to confuse, stories to direct." He continued speaking as he went to the door. "I won't be back. You'll remain here as long as you're reading and drinking tea. Get up, stop reading, and you go back…without knowing everything you should. Usually the champions don't get any forewarning of explanations…but…the other parties are skirting the rules, so we're taking some leeway and skirting them too." He opened the door. "But, absolutely *NO* talking. Talking bad. Understood?"

Violet nodded her head.

"Good. Hope to see you again, but my part in this tale is beholden to rules and other powers."

"Where are you going?" Violet blurted out before he crossed the threshold.

"Nice try," he replied, sticking his head back in the room. "No spoilers. No more talking."

With that, he left, shutting the door behind him.

Violet opened the journal and started reading the first page.

So… here I am…writing Tommy's story before I die.

ABOUT THE AUTHOR

M Todd Gallowglas is a professional storyteller and the bestselling author of the *Tears of Rage* and *Halloween Jack* series.

As a child, Todd wished that he could be a left-handed red head, because he thought they were the most special and different people in the world. As a brown-haired righty, life had forced him to create his own path to being special by making up stories of fantastical worlds of adventure. He even believed in these worlds so completely, that several of his teachers questioned whether he knew the difference between fantasy and reality. The jury is still out.

He wrote his first fantasy story in the third grade. High school was a convenient quiet place to hone the craft of writing adventure stories...while he should have been paying attention in class. Todd received a BA in Creative Writ-ing from San Francisco State University. Throughout his time in at SFSU, several teachers tried to steer him away from writing that nasty "genre" stuff. However, they underestimated how much Todd's brain is hard-wired for tales of the magical and fantastic, and their efforts to turn him to literary fiction came to nothing.

After graduating, Todd returned to his career as storyteller. His first professional sale was to Fantasy Flight Games, and he has a run of stories for their Call of Chthulu game line. His story "The Half-Faced Man" received an honorable mention from the Writers of the Future contest. Embracing the paradigm changes sweeping through the publishing industry, M Todd Gallowglas used his storytelling show as a platform to launch his self-published writing career. Nearly all of his eBooks have been Amazon bestsellers, and *First Chosen* spent most of 2012 on several Amazon bestseller lists.

He currently lives with his wife, three children, more pets than they need, and enough imaginary friends to provide playmates for several crowded kindergarten classes. He is currently corrupting his children by raising them with a rich education of geek culture. And still, as busy as he is, he manages to squeeze in time for some old-school table top gaming and airsoft battles on the weekends (because it's not as messy as paintball). Shiny!

Find out more about M Todd Gallowglas and his books on his official website: www.mtoddgallowglas.com

45477062R00064

Made in the USA
Charleston, SC
23 August 2015